Intergalactic

Was this the key to ι . ---- .

The

ARSENAL

of

MIRACLES

by Gardner Francis Fox

Originally printed in 1964

digitally transcribed 2018 by Kurt Brugel &
Jason Duelge
for the Gardner Francis Fox Library LLC

Illustration by Kurt Brugel

Gardner Francis Fox (1911 to 1986) was a wordsmith. He originally was schooled as a lawyer. Rerouted by the depression, he joined the comic book industry in 1937. Writing and creating for the soon to be *DC comics.* Mr. Fox set out to create such iconic characters as the *Flash* and *Hawkman.* He is also known for inventing *Batman's* utility belt and the multi-verse concept.

At the same time, he was writing for comic books, he also contributed heavily to the paperback novel industry. Writing in all of the genres; westerns, historical romance, sword and sorcery, intergalactic adventures, even erotica.

The Gardner Francis Fox library is proud to be digitally transferring over 150 of Mr. Fox's paperback novels. We are proud to present - - -

Table of Contents:

ONE

IT WAS Bran the Wanderer who found death.

Literally, death: the reason why men must die.

He did not understand what it was he found, at first. Few men would, for it was only a metallic machine set in a city so old its stones turned powdery to the rub of his big hand over them. The machine hummed a little, very faintly, and it was warm to the touch. It appeared to do nothing else.

Bran marveled and walked on.

He had been walking on for several years, ever since he had found the tele-doors, traveling across the wastelands of the star worlds, appearing from out of nowhere on Costair or Uristhinn or Moorn, planets which dotted the crown of Empire which was flung across deep space. He never stayed long in any place. His feet itched for distant sands, for the waters of unseen planets and their high places that only Bran seemed able to find.

After a while he became something of a legend. And then he went to Makkador . . .

He came walking into Makkamar City of its desert sands toward sunset of a day when shadows were at their longest and their blackest and his own shadow, moving in rhythmic stride before him, showed a big man with deep chest and wide shoulders. There was a lean, hard look about him, all over. The dust of the Akkan planets lay on his leotan furs and yellow hair, on the black leather holster of his a-gun. Streaks of dried salt on his boots showed where he had splashed through the waters of half a dozen shallow streams.

A moment he stood on the rim of the gray sands where Makkamar City begins and fingered his belt pouch for the dice he carried always with him. They were strange dice, carved with cats and ships and dragons on solid onyx of a peculiar red color; he had found them in his wanderings; he rarely took a step without rubbing them with the thumb of his right hand and tossing them high.

He did that now, catching them with a side-wise swipe of the hand and opening his fingers to grin down at the twin ships that ran before an onyx wind.

"A lucky symbol, the Kriil ships," he chuckled.

There was a gold coin and three silvery speds in his pocket pouch beside the dice, enough for a feed and a comfortable bed for one night. Bran the Wanderer was wealthy only in his freedom of movement. He had no other riches.

He could eat and sleep with that money. Or–build himself a stake in some space-stews dive. His belly was empty but he had been a gambler too long not to feel a tug from the felt covers he would find on a tavern gambling table.

He needed money, right now.

Why, Bran? To go on roaming to forget Peganna?

Some men found Lethe in the bottoms of their liquor mugs; others, in the women who flocked to the stews. Bran found his in far travels. The sandy world of Conchavar. The great green seas that roll eternally on Slithstan. The high rock mountains of Klard. He had touched them all.

And yet, he wanted more. To see the marsh fires dance their blazing saraband on Duheel. To stare when the copper skies come down on Boharel and kiss the metal trees that are unlike any other trees in the known universe. To walk in the caves of Rann. To climb the Tors on Vomarr. A corner of his mind told him he was a fool, that other men had built new lives from the wreckage of the old. His lips twisted bitterly. None of them had ever known Peganna of the Silver Hair or held her in his arms under the seven moons of Kuleen while wearing the white uniform of Interstellar Fleet Commander.

He snarled low in his throat. "Sure, it's all behind me now. I'm no longer a commander with all his pretty gold braid and precious medals–but a nobody."

A dog ran out of the shadows formed by two buildings where they leaned toward the setting sun as if for a last bit of warmth against the coming cold of night, and barked at him. It was a scrawny yellow hound, a breed called lannx by the men of Makkador, and it looked half starved. As I do myself, Bran thought.

He moved on away from the dog, along a narrow alleyway that twisted halfway across the edge of Makkamar City to its spaceport and the stews that formed a stinking crescent around its launching pads. There would be a thousand taverns in the stews with felt-topped gaming tables. All he had to do was choose one.

At the intersection of two twisting, ancient streets–Makkador was an old, old planet long since lost sight of by Time–he heard the low throb of a star-ship sliding into a vane-down. Bran looked up and felt the breath catch in his throat.

Gods! That gray metal hull had the look of a–but no. The Lyanir design had been copied by some trader, probably. There was no device on it at all, as far as he could see.

Bran shrugged. It was no concern of his, that ship.

He walked under creaking signs swinging on rusted chains in the wind, their painted wood surfaces worn to bareness in spots by the abrading sands of the deserts. One need not be able to read to understand those signs, for each was carved for men to know its meaning, in the shape of a shoe, of a loaf of bread, of a tankard.

He made his choice outside a neatly kept tavern where the cobblestones were broomed and the windows, spotless. A freshly painted pair of benches and a solanthus-wood door told him the food and liquor might be worthwhile investigating.

It was dusk now and the lights were on inside as he laid his palm to the door and thrust it open. The first diners were at the table, the early drinkers were crowding the bar. There was even a handful of men at the low gaming boards. Bran stood a moment on widespread legs sniffing at roasting meat, at tart wine as it flowed from ewers into pewter cups.

On impulse he walked to the green felt table and laid a silver sped on its edge. "One throw of your dice," he said to a bearded *wheen* miner. "A sped against five you can't make your point in as many rolls."

The miner grinned and threw. He threw again and three more times. With a growl he tossed coins to Bran. The Wanderer winked and said, "I'll give you a chance to win them back when I've put meat and wine in my middle."

He rested his rump on a wooden bench and signaled a serving wench to him, ordering meat with gravy and vegetables and a beaker of mead. To his pleased surprise, the food was tasty and hot. He ate slowly, with relish. The meal cost six speds. He had his gold auroch and two speds left with which to gamble. Twelve speds, all told, enough with which to build a new stake for his travels.   He gave the serving maid a pinch on the rump and a kiss on her lips with a promise of twin speds if he proved lucky this night. She told him to keep an eye on the dice of the fat man in the work-clothes of a driller; there were some who said he put weights in them by a method no one had been able to detect. Bran laughed. He had seen all manner and makes of dice in his travels; there were few that could fool his sensitive fingers. But he thanked the girl and unfastened his food pouch, giving it to her to fill with bread and meat and a small task of wine.

Then he moved on the gaming tables.

It took him ten minutes and the loss of his golden auroch to detect the trick of the dice. They totaled seven on adjacent sides so that on a pad roll the sixes faced one another and prevented craps. Once he learned their secret, he built a pile of speds before him until the piles became two in number and then three.

Voices growled around the table. Bran laughed and tossed the crooked dice to the fat man, bringing out his own. He passed them around the table and let the players examine them. He used them until his speds were doubled.

A great crowd had gathered around the boards to watch Bran match his luck with that of half a dozen men. They laughed and made comments between throws but when the dice were rattling around in the leathern cup that one gambler had made Bran use after a while, they held their breaths.

The cup rattled and dipped and the curiously marked dice came rolling across the green baize flashing their queer symbols. "Two dragons of Moorn," shouted Bran and put out a brown hand for the piled coins in the center oval.

"With your luck you ought to try the well of Molween," a half-naked stevedore grumbled.

Bran looked up, intrigued. "Now what do you know of the well? Have you ever seen it?"

The man looked embarrassed. "Someone was asking about it a little while ago, over at the bar. I told him it was a myth, along with that of the six gods of Nomaar, but he insisted it was true."

"Did he now?" Bran asked softly. "And where is this man with the tongue that wags about Molween?"

The stevedore grinned. "Oh, he's gone now. He left when I pointed you out to him and told him only Bran the Wanderer knows where the well is hidden."

"You spoke true words," Bran admitted. "I do know the well. But it's far and far away from Makkador. Across eighty thousand light years of space."

Someone hooted, "No man can go so far in one lifetime, not even with the trans-dimensional drive."

"I can," said Bran and there was truth in the sound of his voice. Men looked at one another and drew back from the table a little. Gossip said Bran was not quite human, that there was an alienness about him, a form of humankind put on to hide a nightmare intelligence from an unknown world. Some men believed the tale.

A brass lamp suspended on its chains from a blackened ceiling beam swung to a cool draft moving through the smoke-filled room as a door opened. A zusthin-skin drum throbbed in the shadows where a crouched changeling drew elemental harmonies from its tightly stretched hide head. A girl sobbed softly in those same shadows, caught up in kleth-induced dreams that shook her ripe body. The swinging lamp laid black shadows on the green felt as Bran leaned over it.

"Well? Does my talk of the well frighten you like little children? Will no one bet against Bran and his lucky dice?"

The brass lamp hissed and the moaning girl quieted. Suddenly the tavern was hushed, for these were the Forbidden Hours of the Serpent on Makkador and only men and women whose lives were as nothing against their lusts and hungers were abroad in the stews. A wind blew the tangy scents of desert weeds in through the barred windows, and with them the smells of old stone buildings and the swill that dotted the cobblestone streets beyond the tavern door.

Bran shook the dice so they made a hollow sound in his cupped palm. "I've won enough for one night, I suppose. Enough to take me off Makkador to some other planet where men will risk a sped or two for an evening's pleasure. Ah, well. It isn't exactly a wasted night, I suppose, with a thousand speds to show for my time but I'd hoped for another roll or–"

"I will play against Bran and his dice of Nagalang."

Silken stuffs rustled in the wind that swirled close to the solanthus-wood door and there was an illusion of bare legs whispering together as they walked. Then a white hand came into the lamplight, a slim hand with green nails. Its fingers opened and three scarlet pearls came rolling across the green felt pad of the gaming board.

A woman stood smiling at Bran. "My flame pearls against your life, Wanderer."

Men drew back before the figure in the spun silk chlamys whose face was hooded against their stare. Eyes sought to probe the cloth edged with purple. Only Bran pretended not to see the gentle curves of hidden hips. He straightened slowly until he towered above the woman and gestured at the leathern cup holding the dice.

His hand was shaking with unaccountable excitement, Bran knew. His heart slammed in its rib cage. The voice that had spoken had come across the void of years–how many years make sorrow in a man for the might-have-been?–and whispered now to the memories in his brain.

Long ago he had heard this voice, long ago and far away in another life. The ripe red mouth that had spoken them he had kissed to breathlessness. The elation in him grew until he was the only man in the room and she the only woman.

Only the senses know reality. His ears and his eyes screamed the truth at him and his hands itched to move out and touch. He controlled himself and made his voice a mockery of what lay deep in his heart.

"My life? What's that against three flame pearls?"

She laughed with melody in her throat, like a sweet charm to give a man dreams. "Those pearls are beyond price. Is your life so valuable?"

A little man with a pockmarked face looked up from the felt pad and the three crimson pearls he had been studying. His bright eyes were feverish with green as he whispered, "Long ago I was court jeweler to Kraad of Palisthan. Once I advised him to buy a flame pearl once worth only half one of these–yet it was the finest gem in all his great collection! With those beauties a man could buy a star system."

Bran did not take his eyes from the features he could see only dimly

10

in the shadow of the white silk hood. "You named the stakes, *si'ilar*," he smiled, giving her a royal title. "If my life is worth so much to you, so be it."

Mocking laughter came to him from the hood. "I choose what you value least, Wanderer. If I win, the manner of your living is mine to name."

He fumbled for the cup, held it out to the white hand with the green nails. "Roll, then."

Her head shook almost imperceptibly. "Yours the first roll, wanderer. Yours is the luck I mean to beat."

Without taking his gaze from the slant eyes that brooded at him from beneath the silken hood, he moved the cup around in his hand, tumbling the dice back and forth inside it. He asked, "How many casts to win?"

"Three. Your point in that time or–you're mine!"

Bran shook his head. "A poor bargain."

But he turned to the green felt and made the dice spin out across its surface so that they glowed with iridescent fires in the lamplight. They showed the dragon crests of Tarrn and the ships of Kriil and then the cats of Bydd. When they stilled on a trio of stars and the banner of the Rim worlds, men sighed.

A *wheen* miner whispered, "The lost stars of Murd and the banner. A bad roll."

"Bad aye!" laughed Bran. "But–for whom?"

His fingers gathered the dice and dropped them one after the other into the cup so they made hollow sounds. He stared deep into the hood, hunting the pale features hidden there and he sighed and rolled again and now the dice showed only a cat and a Kriil ship. Another poor roll. Only with twin dragons could he hope to recoup bad fortune.

"Twin dragons are only an angle away from the cat and the boat," he told the woman, and threw again. The dice gleamed redly in the smoking lamps, red and somehow–evil. They came to rest.

The woman said gently, "The cat and but one dragon. Hand the cup to me, Bran." He started suddenly and half opened his lips to speak but no sound came out; only the breath scratched in his throat to reveal the thoughts tumbling through his brain. He looked down into the leather cup and scowled.

"Eight years ago I was a Fleet Commander in the Empire space navy. I captained the greatest fighting force the Empire ever built. I took Star Force 97 out to meet the Lyanir and smashed them in three battles. They pinned so many medals on my chest for that, I could hardly stand upright."

He held the cup out to the woman whose green-nailed fingers closed about it gently. Bran said, "I rid the Empire of the Lyanir threat. For what I did they took away my command and sat me down behind a desk to handle paper work. All because of a woman."

He heard her sigh. "What woman, Bran?"

"Her name was Peganna. Peganna of the Silver Hair," he murmured as his eyes appeared to hunt beneath her hood.

"Was she so much ill fortune to you?"

He only shook his head, not speaking. She gave a little sigh and turned to the gaming board. The dice rattled in the cup and then she threw and all men watched the rolling Nagalang dice until they settled. Two dragons showed and the woman clapped pale hands.

"I've won, wanderer. That single throw alone was all I needed to own your life."

The hands with the green nails drew the chlamys tighter about her body so that her hips showed round and firm. Fingertips arranged the cowl and now even less of her face could be seen.

The little man with the pocked face; he who had been court jeweler to Kraad, put out a hand toward the dice but Bran was faster. He scooped them up and tossed them high so they winked in the red lamp flames. He caught them deftly, rattled them in his hand, then slipped them back into his belt pouch.

"When do I die, *si'ilar*?" he wondered.

"Who spoke of dying, Bran? I want you alive. Dead, you're of no use to me. You belong to me now, to me alone." Laughter trailed up from the cowl. "Follow at my heels."

There were some who looked to see the Wanderer explode with rage but he only chuckled low and nodded. "At your heels, highborn. Like a hound."

She moved on through the shadows cast by the wall torches, turning to stare back at him from the solanthus-wood doorway decorated with figures of satyrs and running maidens carved onto its hardwood surface. Bran stood for a moment with the red light playing over the white fur of his kilt and brown leather jerkin, his lips twitching into a grin.

"Maybe the dice didn't do me such a bad favor, after all. Maybe the luck they promised is just beginning." He glanced down at the fame pearls on the green tabletop.

"Pick them up. Keep them," said the woman.

He picked them up one by one and held them on his palm, his eyes widening at their ethereal beauty. Living fame was imprisoned in crimson milkiness in those jewels. No man knew whence came the fame pearls or the manner of their making. Here and there, on this planet or that, a man would find one and if he reached a civilized spaceport alive, he sold it for a fortune. These three pearls made the Wanderer the richest man between Earth and Senorech.

The irony of it made him laugh. "To be so rich–yet to be no more than a slave! The humor of the thing tickles my fancy."

His shoulders brushed men aside as he came out of the circle of onlookers around the table. As he stepped close to the woman he saw that the top of her head came to his heart. Eyes watched them, this man whose skin was the color of dull bronze and this woman of whom nothing could be seen but the faint imprint of hips against silk. Bran put out a hand and the door opened. The woman stepped out into the night with the Wanderer at her heels and the door swung shut behind them.

Three moons made bright silver of the fat red surface of ancient Makkador. Pale light flooded the cobbled streets and where it touched the bricks and masonry of the buildings in the su'udar stews, they gleamed as with glowing fire. In the distance, summoning the faithful who worshiped Kronn to the dawn service, a bell tolled mournfully. The wind that had swept the red deserts to the north all night long was dying now in fitful little gusts that powdered the empty streets and stark gray walls of the stone buildings with scarlet dust.

The woman walked swiftly with a feline stride that ate at distance, yet seemed as effortless as the padding of a panther. Bran aped her stride, stalking slightly behind her, a giant of a man whose long yellow hair was caught in a platinum torque in the fashion of the Akkan outlanders. His a-gun thumped its leather holster against his thigh as the white fur kilt swung to his every step.

He waited until the tavern was behind them by five hundred paces. Then he asked, "Why did you come back into my life, witch-woman?"

She walked on until she came to a fountain that had been dry for centuries, turning there and putting back a fold of the cowl to look up at him. "I knew a man once, a man who said he loved me. Yet he believed the lies they told him on Earth and never came back to me as he said he would. I came after him, instead."

His hand went out to her shoulder, caught it through the silken chlamys and held it firmly. Though his clasp must have hurt, she did no more than shiver.

"You violated your agreement. You moved your people off Kuleen."

"And why shouldn't I? You told me to."

"Not I," he said soberly. "You and I knew our agreement. You were to keep the Lyanir on Kuleen as token of your friendliness while I did what I could to induce the Empire to accept you into its hegemony of races."

There was a troubled quaver in her voice. "I kept possession of the 'gram you radioed me. It was signed by you. I knew you well enough– in those days–to recognize your signature."

His sigh was bitter. "Then someone forged it. I sent no 'gram. I was fighting–and winning–a battle to get Empire to give you living room on the Veil planets, empty worlds no one's ever colonized because they're pretty far off the normal trade routes. They'd have been ideal for the Lyanir, far enough from everybody else to give both your people and mine time to get accustomed to the idea of integration without causing incidents by daily shoulder-jostling."

"What happened, Bran?"

His laugh was raw with suppressed anger. "One of the ambitious boys at headquarters got jealous. Evran Dallish, or Alvar Dexter, or David Uronogian. Or–someone else. They were all Commanders, as I was."

"I–I don't understand?"

"What's to understand? One of them decided I was getting too big for my britches. He forged my name and sent the 'gram. When the Lyanir moved off Kuleen to Yvrilis, it was made to look like an attempt to force a quick acceptance of my plan. Empire doesn't like to be threatened. The powers that be decided I'd make a fine teacher for wet-behind-the-ears cadets. They offered me a superintendency of the Academy. I didn't want it and resigned."

"You ran away," she accused.

"I went to find you," he pointed out. "I didn't."

They were standing so near in the shadow of the fountain her thigh pressed into him. The hand that had held her arm so tightly was stroking it now, up to her shoulder and behind her throat, fingers clamping the hood so he could drag it down away from the white face and green eyes and silver hair of the queen of the alien Lyanir. His hot black eyes searched first the red mouth and straight nose and broad forehead where the moonlight touched them. Her long-lashed eyes misted in tears as they stared up at him. When the hood came fully away, her silver hair, long and soft and seemingly filled with pallid fire, was a cloud about the loveliness of her features.

"Peganna," he whispered.

In his memory he tasted the soft moist flesh of her mouth and felt her arms enclosing him as once they had done, so long ago. She stood proud in her white beauty there under the three moons of Makkador while she studied the hard lines on his face with pitying eyes. *We could have had so much, he and I, had not Subb of the Hundred Hates thrust his will upon us!* Sighing gently, she raised the white hood with its fretwork of purple dye and rearranged it about her face.

Eight years before, a race of humanoids who called themselves the Lyanir had swept in toward the Border planets of Earth Empire from the outer stars. In a thousand great star-ships they had crossed the voids between the Tucanae cluster and the Rim planets. Even moving through inter-dimensional space, the voyage had taken them centuries. They were hungry for fresh air, for sunlight, for fresh foods grown in normal dirt and for the taste of natural meat, not its manufactured equivalents.

They had come in peace, contacting the Rim world of Keshabar. In panic, the Keshabar forces had opened fire. The Lyanir shot back. There had been no attempt at negotiation, to arrive at a meeting of human and humanoid minds. Two fleets of the Empire Interstellar Command went out to meet the invaders and were swept into powdery nonexistence by strange rays that acted as does a vacuum on certain metals.

Empire sent its youngest Commander, Bran Magannon, out to meet the Lyanir. Commander Magannon gathered up what he could of the powdered hulks of those first two fleets and ordered the powder analyzed. By driving his Ordnance experts day and night he evolved a metallic compound that the Lyanir rays could not harm.

Once able to get his cruisers within missile range of the alien ships, he wrecked them in a running fight between Keshabar and Kuleen. The name of Bran Magannon was half a legend, already; it had been Captain Magannon who had destroyed the growing power of the sikals on Ceti-21; as Commander Magannon he had shattered the power of the Pumars a million miles outside Fomalhaut. With this latest victory he stood next in line to become Fleet Admiral. His name was a by-word from Earth to Moorn, his fame a toy for small boys to play at winning.

Such success will breed jealousy among both equals and superiors. While Commander Magannon was meeting with the young queen of the Lyanir, Peganna, to discuss surrender terms, Empire officials were making moves behind his back aimed at reducing his stature in the star worlds. It is not easy to smash an idol who has saved a people from defeat in such a way that their money boxes are scarcely opened. Commander Magannon was too fabulous a hero to be destroyed. The best anyone could hope for was dislodgement from his pinnacle which was bathed by stellar spotlight.

The surrender parley went on and on, while Commander Magannon and Peganna of the Silver Hair touched mouths under the skies of Kuleen, dancing nightly above the waters of the Loranian Sea or sipping chilled vinoral on the marble balconies looking out over the Tors. Lost in a world where only his love made sense, he gave his enemies time to perfect their moves.

When Commander Magannon came back from the stars with his Lyanir Treaty worked out to the satisfaction both of himself and young Peganna, his career rivals went to work. Lies and rumors were circulated. His love and friendship for Peganna were distorted into a plot to raise up the Double Ax banner of the Lyanir and create a new empire in the stars, an empire that would see Bran and Peganna become its rulers, an empire which would rival Earth. Forged documents were presented for study to the Tribunal judges even as a raging Bran Magannon lung outraged denials in the teeth of his accusers.

So great was his reputation, so much love had the common people for him, that he might have snatched victory out of threatening defeat had not the Lyanir lifted off Kuleen planet where they had contracted to remain during the treaty negotiations, and gone to Yvriss.

Yvriss sent back word it was being attacked.

No attack was ever made. There had been no bombs dropped or rays beamed down on the peaceful cities of Yvriss. Turned away, the Lyanir fled back into dimensional space, no man knew where. They faded out of existence, seemingly.

Some men said Bran Magannon had ordered their withdrawal, their flight. But there was no proof of this; the Tribunal judges accepted for consideration only the actual facts. They gave Commander Magannon the Solar Cluster and the Star-flare medal, but they put him down on Earth and told him to teach Spatial Warfare at the Academy. In his pride he turned in his resignation, put his uniform and his medals in mothballs, and went out to the stars as a civilian. Somewhere between Earth and the Rim planets, he had disappeared.

Only later, much later, did tales and rumors drift back to his home world of a wanderer who walked alone among the star worlds, who worked at one trade or another until he had enough money to travel on. After a while even those stories faded out; there was gossip that the Wanderer had found a strange and unique way to cross the voids between the stars. He never needed to go by spaceship any more. An archaeology team might sight him on unexplored Dravakian or barren Kaltal, but no one ever saw his spaceship or understood the manner of his coming and his going. He began to play the gaming tables with an odd pair of dice he had found in some forgotten ruin.

The myth of Bran the Lucky had been born.

Now under the three moons of Makkador, he stood once again beside

Peganna of the Lyanir. Her voice as she whispered to him was a dirge for the might-have-been, lost in the night around them.

"We could have had so much, so long ago."

She turned on a heel and walked more swiftly toward the spaceport where twin control towers made a pattern of chrome and glass against the starred sky. Bran went after the white silk of her chlamys as it whipped to her stride in the last few gusts of wind of the desert.

At the edge of the black tanbark, she halted.

"Bran–look!" she cried out, pointing.

He saw the sleek star-ship he had glimpsed hours before, standing bright and silvery in the moonlight. Grouped about its base were men in the white uniforms of the Star Fleet, weapons at the ready.

His arm drew her back into shadows. "Somebody alerted them that yours was a Lyanir star-ship They've put it under guard. They're waiting for you to come back." He felt her shiver against him.

"What does that mean?"

"Officially, you're an enemy of the Empire. I'm a traitor for consorting with you." At that in her pride, she would have pulled free of him but he would not let her go. "Easy! Be easy, girl. I've no intention of letting them come at you. We'll go somewhere else."

"Where, on Makkador? When I don't return to the ship they'll send out searching parties. They'll invade every tavern, every house in Makkamar City. Then they'll start hunting from the air, in Zads. There's nowhere on Makkador for us to hide."

His teeth showed like those of a wolf baring its fangs. "We'll go off Makkador, then–to safety."

She was so startled she cried out as she turned to look up at him. "But how can we, with the spaceports closed? With my ship under quarantine?"

"There are ways I know."

She looked at him queerly but went willingly enough to the tug of his hand at her elbow. They moved back along the narrow alleyways and cul-de-sacs that made the *su'udar* stews a labyrinth of hiding places. Within the hour dawn would flood these cobbled streets and armed details of Fleet soldiers would be patrolling them, hunting the queen of a lost people and the man who loved her.

By dawn, the Wanderer wanted to be far away.

TWO

FLEET COMMANDER Alvar Drexel was angry.

"Where can they be, those two? A woman as beautiful as Peganna and a man as impressive as Bran Magannon–I give him that, freely enough–can't have vanished into thin air?"

His hard stare held his lieutenants rigid. They stood at attention in the Operations Room of the Empire Star-ship *Taliesin*, neatly uniformed in the white action dress of men on an alert. Gold braid sparkled at their left shoulders. Black leather belts snugged their lean middles. Their dress swords hung motionless. They were hard men, fashioned in a tough school, disciplined to a nicety. Not even their eyelids flickered as they waited.

When Drexel raised his blond brows, the shorter man spoke. "We took her ship under surveillance the minute it crossed the Barrier, sir. We've been on alert since twenty hours three days ago, when we had a report that the Wanderer had been seen on Makkador."

"I know all that. You sighted her ship. We passed it through the Barrier without incident, figuring that those two intended a meeting somewhere down below. Well, they met, all right, as we figured, they'd do. Then–we lost them."

"Not lost, exactly, sir. They're down there somewhere. How far can they go? Patrols are moving through Makkamar City, searching it house by house under the Commander's orders."

"That search has been going on for sixteen hours. We haven't turned up a sign of them." Face flushed, Commander Drexel moved to a map case hung along one metal wall. His finger stabbed out to touch buttons.

Maps unrolled too fast for the eyes to follow. The lights slowed after a half minute and firmed. A detailed map of Makkamar City shone on the wall. Alvar Drexel touched it with a forefinger.

"We sent searching parties inward from the four corners of the city. Not one of them has reported catching so much as a glimpse of them. Within the hour those details will make contact at the Square of Krall If Peganna and Bran aren't in this last radius, they aren't in Makkador."

The taller lieutenant said, "Then they're on the desert and not even Bran Magannon can hide from us there. Makkamar City is rimmed by red sand for twelve miles to the north and fifteen to the west. If they try crossing that, our Zads will sight them."

"Suppose they go south to Lunn?"

Polite incredulity showed in the voice of Lieutenant Bradford Madden. "Over fifty miles of red sand? In the heat of Mizar?"

His commander brooded at him. "The odds were greater that Magannon would never defeat the Lyanir, seven or eight years ago. He found a way to do it. He may find a way to get to Lunn."

"And if he does, what can he do? Where can he go? The only spaceport on Makkador is at Makkamar City. Even assuming he came in illegally, as he might with a small spacer, he can't get off-planet without alerting the Barrier."

"Mmmm, yes. I suppose there isn't any real need to worry."

Fleet Commander Alvar Drexel had a very high opinion of Bran Magannon, having been his second-in-command before Commander Magannon had met the Lyanir spaceships in battle. His own wits had been paralyzed at the problem confronting High Command. It had been Bran Magannon alone who had thought to have the drifting debris–all that was left of the Empire war-spacers before the Lyanir rays blasted them–analyzed. When that analysis showed the composition of those awesome rays and when Ordnance found a metallic compound to offset them, he had ridden to a semi-glory on his commander's uniform braids. This dependence rankled in Alvar Drexel.

22

While stationed on Kuleen after the crushing defeat of the Lyanirn and while Commander Magannon spent his hours with Peganna of the Silver Hair, he had made friends of sorts with her brother, young Gron Dhu. Gron Dhu was an ambitious youth. Jealousy of his sister bit in him as jealousy of Bran Magannon bit into Alvar Drexel.

For hours on end they had sipped tart slisthl and conjectured on what might happen if both Peganna and Bran Magannon fell from power. There seemed no hope of this, however, until the treaty terms were agreed upon; then Gron Dhu suggested that, if those treaty terms might be broken and the blame for such breaking laid upon Peganna and Commander Magannon . . .

It was worth a try, they had decided.

Somewhat to the surprise of both, their plan worked. Believing that it was Bran Magannon telling her to rise off Kuleen, Peganna had taken her people toward Yvriss. When they were fired upon, she realized her terrible mistake; by then it was too late to turn back. She had to flee into the void out of which the Lyanir had come to the Rim worlds. And as they fled, Gron Dhu maintained contact with Alvar Drexel, advising him when and where they were going.

Gron Dhu had been silent for seven years. Then he had sent a 'gram on their private wave-length, informing Drexel–now Commander Drexel–that Peganna had left the barren planet where she and the Lyanir had taken refuge. She had a harebrained scheme by which she hoped to compel Empire to give her people shelter, but Gron Dhu knew no more than that. Perhaps if Commander Drexel could manage to intercept her–and Bran Magannon, whom she was hopeful of meeting-he could kill them and make out a case of intended attack on the Empire against them. If this were done, Gron Dhu would make submission to Commander Drexel and together they would work out a deal by which the Lyanir need no longer stay exiled.

If this should happen, Gron Dhu promised to make Alvar Drexel a very wealthy man. During their wanderings between planets, the Lyanir had found fabulous treasures and rumors of others still more amazing. Gron Dhu and Alvar Drexel would share them. No price was too high for the Lyanir to pay for living room, even as subordinates to mankind.

Ten hours ago, Commander Drexel could envision himself living in a mansion on the pleasure world, Nirvalla. Since then, his roseate dreams had been turning a gray, ashen color. If that thrice-damned Bran Magannon and his silver-haired companion should escape–

Alvar Drexel hit his desk with a clenched fist. His two lieutenants blinked at the fury of the blow.

"Send more patrols into Makkamar City. Flood it with searchers. On the double!" His junior officers saluted and ran. Behind them, Commander Drexel worried his lower lip with his teeth.

Where in the name of the Akkan gods could they be?

It was hot walking over the red desert sands with the red wool blankets on their shoulders. From time to time Peganna stumbled and might have fallen had not Bran thrust out his arm to catch and hold her. Fiery Mizar was high in the midday sky, bathing Makkador in heat.

"Luck is with us, Peganna. Hold on for just a little longer." He turned and stared back and upward at the sky behind them. Before any searchers could sight them in their red blankets, he would see the dark dots of their fliers against that pallid sky. Then all he and Peganna need do would be to lie down and cover themselves with the blankets. The red wool would blend with the red sand, and since their prone figures would cast no shadow, they would be as good as invisible.

And in such intense heat as the Makkamar desert, any devices which might locate them by their body-warmth would be ineffective. Bran held Peganna tighter against him and stared northward toward low hills rimmed with stunted evergreens. In those cooler hills with their rocks and many trees, concealment would be easy.

After a little while, Peganna lifted her head from his chest and smiled wearily. "It seems I've been running all my life, Bran. First from the catastrophe that destroyed my home worlds, then across the voids between Lyanol and the Empire planets. From you. From Alvar Drexel when he succeeded to the high command. I'm tired."

He kissed her moist forehead. "Only a few more hours and we'll be safe. Once in those hills we have nothing to worry about."

Her shoulders rounded in discouragement. She shook her head. "Sooner or later they'll find us."

His own voice was grim. "No man can find me if I don't want to be found. Now, how about it? Can you walk?"

She stirred, stretching. Her smile was suddenly buoyant with hope, for the thought touched Peganna of the Lyanir that she really did not mind the ache in her slim white legs so long as Bran Magannon was here for her to lean on every once in a while. Not until she had found him again did she understand how bitterly empty her days had been without him.

She drew the red wool blanket closer about her shoulders, saying, "I'm ready any time you are."

They began striding, side by side.

Since before dawn they had been walking all the way from the su'udar stews. The Wanderer had understood the significance of Empire soldiers stationed about the Lyanir star-ship Fleet Commander Drexel had Peganna under surveillance; he had let her land on Makkador, allowed her to make contact with Bran Magannon. This last he did not know for sure, but he could make a shrewd guess. Someone in the High Counsel of the Lyanir had played the informer. From what Peganna had told him of her preparations for this visit to Makkador, there could be no other answer.

Though he himself suspected Gron Dhu, Bran made no outright accusation to Peganna. On Kuleen, when he had stated his belief that ambition ate too strongly in her younger brother, Peganna had stormed with fury that had expended itself in tears. He would not rouse her displeasure now; he would bide his time. Peganna needed strength for what lay ahead.

Curiosity was strong inside him, but this too, he smothered. Peganna had come out of hiding for a strong reason, yet nothing but the hope to win equality and living room for her people would induce her to place them in danger. Once Empire learned where the Lyanir were hiding, it might send its fleets to destroy them. Peganna must be aware of this; it had been no idle whim that had compelled her to put herself in range of capture and possible torture.

On the other hand, if Commander Drexel had been informed that Peganna was on her way to Makkador, he must also know where the Lyanir were hiding, since his informant would have told him. It was very puzzling.

His eyes slid sideways toward the girl. Somehow she had learned that Bran Magannon was coming to Makkador or was already on that planet. She had come to find him for a reason. What could the Wanderer do to help the Lyanir? Bran honestly did not know.

Nor would he ask until the time was better suited to discussion. He turned and assessed the sky behind him, toward Makkamar City. Long since had its stone towers faded from sight. There was only red desert sand and pale sky to be seen.

No! There to the west. Three dots.

"Get down," he said to Peganna.

She caught the grimness of his voice and obeyed him instantly. She lay flat on her face, the blanket pulled over her so that nothing of her body showed. Bran lay beside her, drawing up his own blanket. He waited until his keen eyes verified his first suspicion; those dots were three Zad-10's, fast interceptor-hunters. They came across the sky almost as swiftly as thought, leaving trails of vapor in their wakes. Their a-motors made no sound. They whispered as they streaked the sky and the sound of their going and that of their detection devices was as silent as the sunlight bathing their vee wings.

Bran waited until they were out of sight before climbing to his feet. Headquarters would be charting the progress of those Zads. Maps would be covered with colored lights to show where they had hunted. They had five hours at least before a re-check brought the fliers back over this northern corner of the desert.

In five hours they would be in the Hills of Dor.

An hour after sunset they were inside a cave that had looked out over this corner of Makkamar desert for uncounted eons. Bran dared not light a fire. A fame could be seen for an incredible distance in the blackness of a Makkadoran night and the Zads were soundless, giving no warning of their coming or their going. For a little while they must endure the cold and the dampness. Warmth would come when Mizar lifted its glowing bulk over the horizon.

Questions burned his tongue, but the Wanderer swallowed them. Peganna was exhausted. The seemingly endless walk over the desert had drained her of energy. Her feet were bleeding; he had been forced to carry her the last few miles. Sleep was what she needed. His curiosity could remain unsatisfied until daylight.

He put his arms about her, held her so the closeness of their bodies would keep them warm, and drew both blankets over them. Peganna rested her silvery head on his chest; Bran was used to a hard rock for a pillow.

"Sleep," he whispered. "Here, you are safe."

He woke twice during the night to gather her even tighter against him. In one sense, Bran cared nothing for the reason that had brought Peganna back into his life; that she was here in his arms was enough for him. If it were not for the danger she was in, he would have been completely happy.

Morning was a redness on his closed eyelids. Bran stirred and felt the weight of Peganna still across his chest. Soft laughter touched his ears

27

and a moist mouth kissed his own. His arms tightened, holding her as she whispered.

"I came hunting you in the hope that we might pick up where we left off, eight years ago. Now I know it can never be."

"Oh? Now what could have changed your mind?" he asked.

She sat up, rubbing her arms against the damp cold of the cave. Thick silvery hair that had come loose of its coif of net pearls in the night, hung down her back to the hard rock. She had never looked so regal, Bran thought, his admiration frank in his eyes for her to see. She flushed and leaning out, put a palm over his stare.

"Not–like this. I'm so rumpled."

"Then be more rumpled," he grinned and would have pulled her down on his chest again except that her face betrayed the despair eating in her. He sat up quickly and caught her hand in his. "Tell me, Peganna. What happened last night to spoil your happiness?"

Her green eyes were feverish with brightness. "The Empire soldiers–oh, Kronn! How I hate the sight of those white uniforms!" Her fingers twisted like snakes within the cup of Bran's hand. She drew a sobbing breath. "I'd planned on contacting you–for a very special reason–when I learned who Bran the Wanderer really was. I sent a thousand spies into the Rim worlds to hunt you down, to bring you to me. The latest rumor said you were somewhere in the Mizar system. To find you, I came to Makkador."

"And very obligingly, I strolled into Makkamar City."

She glanced sideways at him, an elfin smile curving the corners of her mouth. "Makkador was the fifth planet I vaned down on, Bran. You had to be on one of the Mizar planets if that rumor was correct. And it was."

"All right. You've found me. Why?"

"I ought to be insulted by that, Bran Magannon," she stated, pretending indignation. "If you really loved me you'd never say such a thing."

"It wasn't merely love that made you seek me out," he commented wryly, then at her pout he laughed and caught her in his arms. Bran held her until she begged him to ease the pressure of his arms so she might breathe.

"Men said the Wanderer had seen many strange things in his travels," she murmured when she could.

"Marvelous things, sights no other man has ever beheld."

He nodded soberly. "A thousand miracles hidden in far space, on planets so distant man will take a hundred centuries to reach them."

Her eyes flickered. "Yet you found them."

His white teeth glistened in a grin. "I found them," he said flatly, "only because I know a way to travel without a spaceship."

Ah, that shook her! She thrust back from him and put a hand to her silver hair, pushing it away from her glittering green eyes. Bran feasted his eyes on her pale white features. By Kronn, she was a beautiful woman! The years had only ripened her, giving her willowy younger body the sweet curves of maturity.

"Without a spaceship?"

"By tele-doors. Teleportation. Oh, Empire scientists have been working on it a long time, and they've succeeded to a minor extent, but the doors through which I walk were built by a master race, a race of beings so far ahead of us in scientific concept that–"

As he shook his head, he felt the green nails of her hand bit into his arm. "The Crenn Lir–or so at least we call them," she breathed.

Bran blinked. "You know about the Crenn Lir?"

Excitement made her rise to her feet and move up and down the cave in that feline walk that was a mark of all her people. Her cheeks were flushed, her breasts trembling with the emotion powering her faster heartbeats. She went to the door of the cave and stood staring out at the blazing sky and scarlet desert stretching everywhere.

"Once the Lyanir inhabited the planets of a star system many thousand of light years from Earth, as you know. Avan, you named our star-sun. Long ago there was a disaster of almost incomprehensible magnitude on the edge of another galaxy. Had not a billion light years separated that catastrophe from our worlds, we'd have been wiped out of existence within the wink of an eye."

Bran nodded. "Radio telescopes on, Earth picked up evidence of that explosion back in the twentieth century. Men said then that a force was released instantaneously, equivalent to all the energy generated by a billion Sols from their birth to their end as star-suns. It must have been a fearsome thing, whatever it was that happened."

She nodded, framed in the cavern entrance. "So fearsome that even on Lyanol it meant death to everyone unless we could go away."

"You built a thousand great spaceships."

"Yes. In them we put what we could of our culture and all the people who could go. It was a scientific selection. Only the youngest and the ablest were chosen, My great-great-grandfather was rayanor then, as I am reyanal now. They set out across space, traveling inward through our galaxy."

"A long trip," Bran said quietly.

"You cannot know how long. The journey lasted several centuries. At the beginning our ships were not equipped to travel in hyperspace. It took a century even with everyone in the ships working on the project to develop such a means of movement. After that we made better time."

She turned and smiled back at him. The sunlight in her long hair made it gleam like molten gold. "We paused from time to time to live a little while on such worlds as had an atmosphere. Usually they were barren planets, burned out as though by some terrible force."

"And on every one of them you found evidence of an ancient civilization, that of the Crenn Lir."

Her eyes opened very wide. "You've been on them–on some of them at least!" she cried.

"I told you I had. I've wandered far from the usual haunts of men, Peganna. I tell myself I've learned a wisdom of sorts, seeing those other worlds where no feet but mine have raised the dust in perhaps a million years or more."

"On any of them–did you find the well of Molween?"

He came off his rump and went to stand before her, putting his hands at her elbows, staring down fixedly into her eyes. "Last night at the tavern a man mentioned the well. To the men of the Empire, Molween's well is only a myth, a fairy-tale of space."

"Like all myths, at some time it had a reality of sorts."

"How did you learn of the well?"

Her lips twisted bitterly. "As I've said, we Lyanir have had time to do many things with nothing else distracting our minds. To learn the mechanisms of the hyperspace drive, for one thing. To develop a weapon to protect us against attack, the oradirays which you solved, for another. And–to break the language barrier of the Crenn Lir"

It was Bran's turn to start. "You did that?" he asked softly and in his voice was the excitement of a man seeing a dream come to life before his eyes. He said swiftly, "Peganna, these people you call Crenn Lir built the tele-doors. I'm almost positive of it. Long and long ago they came and went by way of the doors to this planet and that. It may be that your race and mine are descended from them, that Lyanol and Earth, and some of the other inhabited planets which men found when

31

they could travel to the stars, are remnants of Crenn Lir colonies."

He paused reflectively. "We have a racial memory of a time when there was no need to toil, when the beasts and man could converse with one another. By telepathy? Religious books have called it Eden."

Peganna smiled wanly. "Our forefathers named it Aesann."

"How did you break the language?" he asked.

"We made everyone work on it, even the little children. On our journey inward across space to your Rim worlds, we stopped at several of what once had been Crenn Lir planets. We found old ruins crumbling to nothingness in the wind. We made three-dimensional pictures of them and built scale models. Naturally, every fragment of language or pictograph we found we photographed.

"At first only our philologists worked on the problem. We had no common denominator–as you've told me Earth once had with the Rosetta Stone that enabled your philologists to to learn the language of the ancient Egyptians."

"And later, the Aradnae stele which helped the early solar system explorers to understand High Martian."

Peganna nodded. The warming breeze off the desert blew her silken jersey and kilt against her body and stirred the long silver hair. It was hard to think of her as a queen of the Lyanir. To him she was only the woman he loved come back to him.

She went on, "After you defeated us and went to Earth to draw up the treaty which would allow us to live in peace with the Empire, and I foolishly believed the lying message that said you wanted me to take the Lyanir to Yvriss–we fled back to those ancient Crenn Lir worlds.

"We suspected that theirs was a scientific culture many levels above our own. We decided in counsel that if we could break their language we might come up with some sort of wedge with which to pry living room from the Empire. We made a national field study of the Crenn

Lir language, with our philologists trying to make linguistic experts of us all."

"You had a little more than seven years in which to do it," Bran said slowly, "while I was wandering between the stars."

"And we did it, Bran. We learned the meaning of those little squiggly characters that made up the Crenn Lir language."

Bran grinned. "For that gift alone, Empire ought to accept you into its hegemony."

Swiftly she shook her head. "No, it isn't enough. Not nearly enough. The Lyanir must learn how to compel the Empire to give it what it wants. Peacefully, if we can. If not peacefully, then by superior methods of waging war."

"Peacefully," Bran said soberly. "I've seen enough warfare."

She nodded, touching his jawline with quivering fingers. "Yes, by peaceful means, Bran. If it can be done that way. But it must be done, in any event. Our children grow thin and weak for lack of proper foods. Manufactured proteins and carbohydrates can do only so much. They need warm sunlight instead of the weakness of dying stars, the fresh breezes of honest atmospheres instead of air that has been tainted with a hundred forgotten nuclear wars."

Her people had suffered much, displaced as they were from their home worlds, forced to struggle against the uninhabitability of dying planets and the indifference of the Empire to their needs. Sympathy was warm and alive in Bran Magannon. He was an Empire man, trained for most of his years under the aegis of the Star Cluster, but the human part of him went out to the Lyanir. They were human, too. Brothers of a kind, if the Crenn Lir were their common ancestors.

"I know your needs," he reminded her gently. "I fought for them in Counsel. And I'd have won my point, if you hadn't come off Kuleen and moved on Yvriss."

"Who sent that message telling me to go to Yvriss, Bran? Who wanted the Lyanir to be homeless and without friends?"

"I don't know." His big hand doubled into a fist. "I've wished I did– so many times I've lost count of the number."

"Perhaps it's just delayed it," she exclaimed hopefully. "As I say, we learned the language of the Crenn Lir. Slowly, but steadily. We found a metal tablet listing the names of the star worlds which were a part of the Crenn Lir monarchy. Erased by time, we made them live again by special rays that penetrated the old metal. One name was recognized as an old, old term in the Lyanir language. It meant 'home' to us. It was a beginning.

"Here and there we made other strides. We began to dig on the dead planets where we vaned down. Sometimes we uncovered bits of pottery, of metal, of stone with symbols inscribed on them. Our archaeologists matched them up with microfilm records of the stars where the Lyanir had lived.

"One word became seven, then fifty, then a hundred and eighty. Now we made very rapid progress. Soon we could read the Crenn Lir language almost as well as our own. And from a room that we believe was once a part of the Crenn Lir military setup, we learned about the well of Molween."

She laughed a little. "Only they didn't call it that. They had a special name for it. Drahusban, which means in our tongue, supply depot."

"Supply depot?" he repeated.

Her white hands clapped together. "You're a military man, Bran Magannon! What's the one thing that must always slow down an army on the move?"

"Its base of supplies, where it can get the food, the ammunition, the weapons, medical care and other provisions it needs to keep functioning at top level. A slow supply train means a slow army, which in turn usually spells defeat."

His eyes widened. "Then if the Crenn Lir discovered a portable supply base they could carry always with them–and if that base worked by teleportation as did their tele-doors–then they solved the toughest problem in making war."

"Such is the well of Molween," she nodded.

To the Empire worlds, the well of Molween was a myth out of space-lore It ranked with all the old Earth fables, with the waters of immortality, the lamp that granted wishes, the flying horse, the enchanted sword. Was there more than folklore to this well of Molween, then? As there might be more to the old beliefs that once men had been immortal, that there were weapons that could never be rendered ineffective? There was a school of thought that said myth was no more than an ancestral memory of past reality.

The collective unconscious, one psychologist had named it. Back on Earth in the old days, Troy had been thought to be no more than a legend. Schliemann had dug in Asia Minor and uncovered its actuality. The same with Crete and the Minotaur, the flood, the hanging gardens. A man named Jung claimed that the wisdom of all time lay hidden in the human mind.

Might that hidden memory extend even to the eons before man had walked the Earth? If Earth had been a colony of the Crenn Lir at one time, its fable of a wishing well might prove to be more than imaginative invention.

"We knew about the wells," Peganna was saying, "but we could never find one. When some of those thousand spies came back to me, telling me about Bran the Wanderer and the stories he told of his findings far out in space, I began to put two and two together. Perhaps you had found one of these wells. If you had, our knowledge of the Crenn Lir language might be enough to activate one of them."

Bran shook his head dubiously. "After so many years–eons, almost– the wells will be dead. Inoperative."

"Perhaps. And perhaps not. Is it worth a try?"

Bran nodded, staring out across the desert sands. "Yes, of course. If you wish, I'll take you to the well of Molween."

She followed his gaze out across the red wastes. "You mean, if the Empire soldiers don't stop us."

"We don't have far to go," he muttered. "For the most part, we can keep off the desert. We're in the hills now and the trees will afford good shelter. No, I don't think Empire will be able to prevent our leaving Makkador."

Her hand slipped between his fingers, clinging. "Then let us go, Bran. It frightens me, being so close to where men in those white uniforms can seize me."

"First we eat," Bran told her, lifting out bread and meat from his food pouch, blessing the foresight that had made him tell the serving woman at the tavern in Makkamar City to fill the leather bag for him.

They sat cross-legged near the cave entrance and munched slowly, wondering when and where they might eat their next meal. From a small flask, Bran poured tart wine. From time to time he glanced out at the empty sky and desert sands, asking himself how close the Empire soldiers might have come in the night.

After a while he took out the Nagalang dice and began to rub them thoughtfully with his thumb.

THREE

THEY WAITED in the lessening shadows while Mizar climbed the distant skies, flooding Makkador with heat. It was a quiet, contemplative moment for them both. Peganna thought of her people waiting patiently on the worn-out planet they had called home for the past seven years, and her heart hungered to give them a pleasant, grassy world heavy with sweet water and hot sunshine. A world that belonged now to the Empire. Bran Magannon was remembering that he was an Earthman, a one-time Fleet Commander sworn to uphold the star cluster of the Empire against all foes. To his world, this woman standing beside him was an enemy, her people a threat to the security of his own.

Bran sighed and tightened the belt of his fur kilt. For the past half hour the sunlight had been moving across the stone floor of the cave entrance until now it almost touched his boot. It was time to leave the cave and venture into the brilliant light of Mizar.

He rose and lifted Peganna from the stone floor. He gathered and folded the blankets, draping them across one shoulder. The pouch at his belt was shrunken in upon itself, and he wondered if this might be symbolic of their chances. Shrugging off a momentary despondency, he caught Peganna by the hand and drew her with him out of the cave.

The skies were empty of Zads, the desert of soldiers.

Bran led the way up a sloping rock to a higher level where dirt lay piled in rock crannies, nourishing the evergreen life of the Makkadoran hills. Pine needles carpeted the rocks and the ground about them, making a cushion for their feet. Sunlight splotched tree boles and underbrush where it filtered through the high branches. It was a silent world through which they walked, hushed but for their own breathing.

When Mizar was overhead, Bran paused and made Peganna sit on a flat rock. "We cross an open space half a mile beyond this point. We'll

37

have to move fast in case there are Zads out hunting us. Rest a while."

He stared south and east in the direction from which they had come. The skies were clear. Though he knew and reckoned with the speed of those feet searching planes, he felt for the first time that they might actually escape the manhunt. Once let them get off Makkador and he would lose the Empire soldiers with ease.

When they came to the two miles of open rock that lay between the evergreens and the tall pines higher in the hills, he scanned the air again. Peganna watched him, thinking. On this man rested all her hopes, not only for her own happiness but also for the future well-being of the Lyanir. He was no Lyanirn, however, but an Earthman. His loyalties should lie with Empire in any conflict between their races–and their disputation over living room on decent planets might well come down to open war. In fact, it probably would, she thought gloomily. Even supposing that the well of Molween might give her what she needed, she had no guarantee that the Empire would buckle to her demands.

Peganna slipped off her silken chlamys. She could run faster in the wool jersey and short, matching kilt that left her white legs so bare. The chlamys was rolled up and tucked into her belt when Bran swung around to her, nodding. "Run, Peganna. Run fast. I'll match your pace."

They almost made the distant trees. They moved swiftly, holding their breaths as long as they could, their shadows keeping pace beside them. It was another shadow–a dark moving blotch that came and went so fast that Bran almost did not see it–which alerted him to danger.

"Fall flat, fall flat," he cried. When he touched the rock he rolled so that his eyes would be staring upward into the bright blue sky.

He did not see it at first, the Zad was so high. Only a vapor trail betrayed its presence. It was gone even while he looked. No living man could have picked them out on the gray rocks, but the reconnaissance camera would be clicking from the underbelly of the

Zad and its high-speed films would catch them as they ran, mirroring forever the fact that they had flung themselves upon the hill stones.

When they processed the films, they would know where they had come, though they would not know why. Bran was thoughtful as he scrambled to his feet. These hills would be swarming with white uniforms in an hour, maybe even less.

By that time he must be at the tele-door and through it with Peganna. Or everything they were fighting for would vanish like smoke in a high wind.

"The Zad's gone," he rasped. "Come on!"

She staggered the last few feet and only his arm at her middle kept her upright. From overhead the tree branches embraced them in dark shadows, hiding them from further discovery. Bran let Peganna lean against a tree-bole to recover her breath while he told her what he had seen.

"They'll be here as soon as they've seen those films. By then, we'll be far away."

"Through the tele-door?"

He nodded. "I'll have to hide the opening I made when I came through it onto Makkador. Even then I'm not sure they won't be able to track us. They have marvelous devices for hunting out a man they want, the intelligence services. Odd little gadgets that can follow a scent the way no bloodhound ever could."

Peganna shivered and, unrolling her white chlamys, thrust her head and arms into its hood and sleeves. Beneath the trees it was cool. Putting back the hood she let that coolness lave her face while she slowly recovered her strength.

"All right," she told him after a few minutes. "We might as well go on. If there's any chance at all of losing them, let's take it."

They walked between the trees toward a high rounded hill where only sparse vegetation grew. There was a small black circle at the base of the hill. When they came nearer, it became the entrance to a tunnel, with charred splotches at its edges.

"The tele-door is under the hill," Bran explained. "When I came through it, I found the exit blocked by the accumulated silt of ages. I burned a way out with my a-gun."

Peganna had become archaeologist enough, during the searching of the Crenn Lir worlds, to recognize a tell when she saw it. Usually these tells covered grave sites or cities so ancient they had long since been buried under many feet of loam. The tele-door would be such an artifact, brooding here on Makkador for unremembered centuries as the detritus from space and the drifting dust from its own planet slowly buried it.

Bran was saying, "Many tele-door chambers are hidden underground, beneath tells or simply to protect them from discovery by enemies. This isn't the first one I've had to shoot my way out of." He reached for her hand to help her scramble up the dirt ziggurat. The black tunnel mouth was perhaps twelve feet above them.

"Long ago there was a staircase of sorts descending from the chamber," he told her. "This one's buried under loess, but others on different planets can be seen, and they all seem to conform."

He had paused to drop the blankets, knotting two ends together to make a drag with which to obliterate their footprints. "To make it a little harder to find us," he explained.

His palm pushed her into the tunnel while he stood in its mouth and began to claw down dirt to fill the entrance. Over his shoulder he said, "I won't be able to do more than disguise it a little. Working from inside, I can't hide the depression it will make. It'll be spotted easily enough if anyone knows what to look for."

"And if they find the entrance–and the tele-door?"

Bran shrugged. "Then they'll come after us."

He worked swiftly, knowing that time was a changeling ally. His fingers grew grimy but the dirt began filling up the adit, so that soon only a narrow space remained through which the outside light could enter. Within moments this was gone and they were in a darkened tunnel.

"Go on, straight ahead," called Bran, working with the a-gun now, blasting down the ceiling of the tunnel, filling it with heavy dirt-slides He backed slowly before the flaring blue beam from the handgun. As he had shot his way out of the tunnel chamber, now he pulled it down behind him. The tunnel was filled with the acrid reek of atomic disintegration powder.

When his rump touched the cold bronze of the chamber doors he stepped into a rectangular room, putting his left hand to each door and swinging it shut. He heard the faint click of an automatic lock.

Peganna was staring around the chamber in awe.

"We've never found anything so well-preserved," she breathed.

She ran to a mural that showed an ocean and an odd sailing craft cleaving its green waters. Gently her fingertips reached out to that brightly colored surface that had been created untold centuries before. Her hand hesitated in midair, then fell away. Almost shamefacedly she turned to smile at him.

"I'm afraid to touch it. The slightest contact might turn those paints to powder and obliterate them." She whispered, "If only I had a camera, to record that scene."

She found a trace of words painted in a lower corner and bent to study them. " 'A skiff on the ocean called Palandrus on the planet Keethan, the world where Thruul was born," she translated.

Straightening, she said, "A skiff, I translated this word, *coelzin*. Our archaeologists have long known what the word meant, though we had no visual image of the boat it represented."

"This must be a scene out of their far past," Bran told her. "I've seen other murals on other worlds where their boats were driven by rockets."

Peganna nodded, turning to study the painting of a vast city in the air above which queer vessels sped like wheeling birds. "Vasthor," she whispered. "Vasthor, that was the Crenn Lir center of learning and culture. We always thought it a fabled place, but apparently it actually existed. Oh, Bran if we could find it, uncover just a few of the wonders it's supposed to have housed!"

He caught her by an arm. "We have no time for that. Maybe someday, but right now we'd better get out of here."

Bran brought her toward a glistening black oval set flush against the far wall, bordered by an edging of what looked to be dull gold. As they came nearer, Peganna, expected to see her reflection; instead there was only a dark emptiness, as though she stared into space itself unrelieved by starlight. It was frightening. She seemed to stand on the edge of a bottomless abyss.

"Step forward," Bran said.

"Oh, no!"

She drew back against him, trembling. To step forward into that dark nothingness was beyond the power of her muscles. She could not; her legs were quivering and refused to move. She would drop into an abyss without bottom in an endless falling that–

Strong arms swung her upward.

Bran held her firmly as he walked lightly and easily through the dimensional blackness of the tele-door. He did not know what the darkness was, though he suspected it was an as yet unknown-to-mankind form of trans-spatial energy. It was everywhere in that black dimensional-continuum and as soon as an animate or inanimate object came within its mutronic flow, he or it was borne elsewhere by its current.

Somehow, the Crenn Lir had discovered that odd type of energy and learned to control it. He himself had been on upward of sixty dead planets which once had formed the star empire of the Crenn Lir, but he always felt that he had only set foot on a small number of their worlds.

He stood an instant in darkness.

Then the blackness formed a roseate oval before him and he stepped through it onto the glassite floor of a chamber he had never seen before. It was a huge room, ornate with many carvings, with several tele-doors set flush to its walls.

He made a mental note of the spatial coordinates so that when he was entering a tele-door with controls–there had been none on Makkador– he would be able to find his way back.

From Makkador, the soldiers of the Empire, if they found the tele-door, would be teleported here. They might remain and hunt for Bran Magannon and Peganna of the Silver Hair, but their quarry would be far away by that time. Bran touched the control discs set into the wall beside a tele-door,
working them from memory.

Peganna stood beside him, saying nothing, a little overwhelmed by what she was seeing all around her. This tele-chamber was something of an art gallery as well, filled with statuary graven in stone and worked in metals, in free form concepts of dead thought and imagery that went on living while their creators were less than dust. Beyond the statues were other works of art. Her breath caught at their beauty– murals and hanging pictures which showed a world long since forgotten by the living. And a row of tele-doors with their sidewalls covered with discs and tiny dials were unspoken passwords to what had been the Crenn Lir empire, where other such treasures might be found!

If only she could turn her scientists loose in this room!

Perhaps there would be no need to force the Empire into granting them living room. Surely among all the old Crenn Lir worlds, there were some still fit for human habitation! Pleasant worlds with grass and flowing rivers and tossing oceans and burning, healthful sunlight.

Bran said, as if reading her mind, "There are none left. Peganna. Whatever force destroyed one, destroyed them all. It was a great tragedy."

She glanced at him sideways. "By that you mean you've never found any. I can't believe all of them were made unfit for living purposes."

He shrugged. "There may be some. If they exist, why haven't we heard from their peoples?"

"What about Makkador?"

"I don't believe Makkador was a true Crenn Lir planet. It may have been explored by them, perhaps marked for colonization. But for some reason the Crenn Lir never got around to it. For that matter, what of the world your people live on now?"

"Miranor? It's a dead planet. Worn out. Bathed as are all the Crenn Lir worlds by some deadly radiation. We have to take medipills two or three times a day to ease its effects on our bodies. Without the pills we'd die out in a few years."

"As the Crenn Lir died out?" Bran wondered.

Peganna only shook her head and allowed Bran to take her by the hand and lead her into the tele-door. She was no longer afraid. Whatever force had gripped the Wanderer and held him upright would also support her.

There was no sensation within the blackness. It closed about her and cradled her gently, as might a suspension beam. Then the roseate oval was in front of them and with Bran's palm at her back she moved toward it.

44

This chamber was small, almost dingy. The almost eternal uthium lights which had made the other chamber gleam with brightness were dull here, almost inert. She supposed the chamber with the statuary had been an important one; this room where she walked now might have been only a mere way-station.

"We aren't going to stay here," Bran told her, "but there's something I want you to see outside the tele-doors–the machine on the Crenn Lir worlds that still works."

Her curiosity was caught at once. Her every hope for her people was based on the assumption that somewhere in space she could find ancient artifacts of the Crenn Lir, a few of their formidable weapons. Perhaps this machine that Bran spoke of might be what she needed.

"Oh, yes," she breathed. "Let's go look at it."

The same type bronze doors through which they had entered the tele-door chamber on Makkador were here. Bran pushed them open and sunlight flooded the room. Peganna shaded her eyes as she looked out over a landscape charred black as by some olden cataclysm. She saw gray rocks thrusting up through the ruined ground, but nothing else. No bit of color, no bud or leafy thing broke the dead monotony of the blackness and the rocks.

Only in the distance . . .

She turned to look up at Bran. "Is it one of their cities?"

"What's left of it. The machine is there."

"I want to see it, Bran. So much!"

He nodded, and they set off across the dead landscape. It was a depressing place, all gray rock and charred ground. No life of any sort existed here, as far as he knew. No intelligent beings or animals trod its surface. The destruction that had overtaken this planet had been a most deadly one.

As they walked, Peganna shaded her eyes while she blinked up at the sun. It was a red giant that filled half the sky but gave only a comparatively feeble warmth for all its size. She commented on this and asked its name.

"I haven't the faintest idea," he told her. "I stayed here overnight once, just to see the star patterns. There weren't any. Only *two* stars were visible."

"Only two?"

"I had no telescope, just my eyes."

"But–no stars!"

"It must be a very remote planet," Bran reflected, "set so far from the other Crenn Lir worlds as to be on the very perimeter of its empire."

"Maybe this wasn't a Crenn Lir world at all."

"Perhaps, though the architecture of the city resembles theirs. My own belief is that this was once a distant Crenn Lir planet, the one most remote from its fellows and most liable to attack by an enemy. None of the other planets I've been on have this charred look."

Black dust rose about their calves as they walked. The air was fresh, the wind gentle. Whatever tragedy had overtaken the planet–Bran had named it Deirdre of the Sorrows, he told Peganna–was lost in the folds of Time. Any radioactivity or other deadly after-effects had been dissipated long ago.

The city grew larger to their eyes. In olden times it had been a mighty metropolis. Now it was only a pile of rubble extending for many miles. Tumbled stones lay like giant play blocks standing on end or lying on their sides. Here and there part of some ancient tower rose upward like the finger of a dead colossus buried amid the debris. They found the shattered remnants of a road after a while and this made walking easier.

Soon they were in the outskirts of the city. Up this close the building blocks proved to be gigantic, carved by super-normal means out of solid granite. Here and there they could detect the outlines of massive buildings, even the twisted remains of a metal object, distorted by an unimaginable force into an unrecognizable mass of metal.

"It's so gloomy, so sad," Peganna whispered.

"Deirdre of the Sorrows," nodded Bran. He smiled down at her. "Or don't you know your Irish history?" He told her a little of that Irish maiden who had unwittingly caused the death of so many fine men and brought tears to the eyes of Ulster women. "Can you think of a better name for such a place?"

She shook her head, reflecting on the desolation which must have come upon this world during the terrible holocaust that destroyed it. Her sadness seemed to penetrate her body, creating a rhythm with her thudding heart before she realized this throbbing came from an outside source.

Bran touched her arm, pointing. "See there, Peganna."

It was a great cube of shining metal that looked like highly polished steel. Fifty feet high, it was equally wide and equally long. It gleamed brightly in the sunlight and from it came the dull throbbing that formed an ache in the ears after a while.

Bran walked up to it, laid the flat of his hand against it. "It's smooth and warm and something inside is pulsing away steadily . . . without stop, without pause."

Peganna came up beside him and put her white hand beside his brown one. Now she could feel warmth and the sound that seemed trapped inside. There was no break in the metallic sides, no sign of an opening, even of a slit into which the edge of so much as a bit of paper might be thrust.

"What is it?" she wondered. "Has it any purpose?"

"I thought you could tell me, since your people learned the Crenn Lir language."

Her silver hair quivered as she shook her head. "There was no mention of any such machine in the writings we saw. Of course, most of our translations were done from stone fragments. This machine might be a more recent invention, so recent that there was no public acknowledgment of it graved in stone. And every other writing material seems to have perished with time."

Bran let his eyes assess the humming metal square. "It must serve a purpose. It's been working now for a million years, I'd guess. Or however long it's been since the Crenn Lir planets were destroyed."

"And maybe before that. Maybe this is what powers the tele-doors." She glanced at Bran. "Someday I want to come back, Bran, to study this more closely. But right now–I'm more interested in the well of Molween."

"Molween is far away. We'd best go back to the tele-door."

They turned and walked away. In their footprints black dust. stirred and shifted, then settled down to its eons-old rest.

The great machine hummed on.

FOUR

THROUGH THREE black doors and two roseate ovals Bran and Peganna traveled before they put foot on the planet Molween. The Crenn Lir had another, unknown name for this world; Molween was an Empire term given it by an explorer five hundred years before who had vaned down on its surface after coming out of hyperspace. In those days, before the invention of the hyper-spatial compass, men had no way of knowing where in space they would emerge from that misty universe through which man first traveled to the stars. It was a hit or miss proposition all the way.

Twice since then had men set foot on Molween, each time returning to confirm the story told by that initial explorer. There was a well on Molween. It did grant wishes, after a fashion. What a man asked for, the well gave, the men said.

One man told of a needed bearing for a damaged motor that the well supplied. Another said he asked for gold, and produced a golden ingot as proof of what he claimed. They always added that the well did not grant every wish, for some reason, only an occasional one. But it was enough to begin the legend.

"Did you make a wish, Bran?" asked Peganna as they emerged from the tele-door into a small chamber in the walls of which were set dioramic displays behind glass panes.

"I did. I asked for a map of the planet. There wasn't any answer." He paused, waiting for Peganna who stood staring into a dioramic display of green desert across which a tiny deer fed before a pack of howling dune wolves. She murmured, "The law of the universe. The strong destroy the weak." Her chin firmed as she swung on him. "I intend to be weak no longer, Bran Magannon."

He nodded understandingly. "The Empire Counsel only understands a show of force, at times."

Her eyes never left his face. "I intend to ask the well for a weapon, a weapon against which there is no defense."

"I hope you get it."

She moved ahead of him, hips swaying, toward the bronze door that opened to the touch of her palm so that she went out into the sunlight and stood a moment breathing in crisp, cool air. She made a wistful picture in her white chlamys with its hood thrown back so that her silver hair blew free about her white face. *She is so small to be a queen, so lonely and so lovely.* In his heart he cursed the stupidity of officialdom that had denied her people the right to live among them, to become a part of Empire.

He wondered if a weapon would help her.

She walked ahead of him down metal steps to broad grasslands stretching away toward the horizon, broken only here and there with stands of tall, stately trees. Molween had survived the disaster that had overwhelmed her sister planets in rather good fashion, Bran thought. All it seemed to lack was people.

When he mentioned this to Peganna, suggesting that her people come here, she shook her head. "We tried a few of the Crenn Lir planets and found there is an unknown force that makes us ill, very ill. Almost as if a curse still hangs over the Crenn Lir worlds."

"I never felt it," he said.

"You never stayed long on any one planet, Wanderer. The force never had a chance to build up in you."

"And on Miranor, where your people now live?"

She shrugged. "The force is weak. We've developed drugs that counteract its effects for a little while. But to go on like that is intolerable. This is a period of marking time for the Lyanir, Bran. Until I find what I want from the well of Molween."

Thcy walked across the grasslands with the wind blowing sweet and clean in their faces. Bran Magannon realized that he felt fully alive for the first time in years, walking here with the woman he loved. It was as if, by not being near her, he had been half dead. When they were under the shadows of a tree, he put a hand on her arm and drew her back to him.

He kissed her hungrily, thrilling to the softness of her mouth. She trembled in his arms like a wild thing in the hands of a hunter.

"Bran, I'm so afraid. So afraid!"

There were tears in her eyes; he kissed them away while she sobbed laughter. "I'm so alone, so alone," she whispered.

"Not now. Not with me beside you."

"But you're an Earthman. Not a Lyanir."

"I'm a man, first of all. My first duty is to the race of men whether they wear the star cluster of Empire or the twin axes of Lyanol."

Her eyes glowed up at him. "Oh, Bran! You mean that, don't you? Knowing you're with me all the way means so much. So much!"

He grinned at her, still locking her in the grip of his arms. "Did you honestly doubt me? While men like Alvar Drexel control the Intergalactic Fleet for Empire, I want no part of it. My hope is that by uniting the Lyanir with the men of Empire–we can make something better than either."

"To do that, we need a weapon to compel Empire to accede to our demands." She said it almost as a question, looking up into his eyes.

"It's the only thing I can think of that will put the fear of the Lord in them. And to force the Empire to do something, you've got to shake them up pretty badly."

Her hand caught his, warm fingers gripping him tightly. "Then come on, Bran. Come on!"

Laughter trailed from her lips as she ran through the high grasses like a wood nymph. Just so had she been those years before on the treaty planet, Kuleen. Bran sorrowed for the years they had been apart and ran with her.

In the distance now they could see the topless towers of a Crenn Lir city. There was no char of ruin here as there had been on Deirdre, however. The buildings of this world had crumbled in upon themselves with age. There was an air of desolation about them that came with abandonment, not with destruction.

"It's as though the people living here just packed up and went away," Peganna murmured as they moved across the smooth streets.

"Or—died of," he growled.

"As suddenly as all that? Leaving everything almost as it had been while they were alive?"

"Something like that, yes."

She eyed him wonderingly. "What could possibly cause such a thing? Neither Empire nor the Lyanir know a power as great as that."

"I know, I know. It's what worries me."

She seemed startled but only tightened the grip of her hand on his as they walked. There was a new eagerness in her stride, reflecting the troubled attitude of her thoughts.

Then the buildings on either side of them opened to a great square where once had been set metal rods and chains connecting them, surrounding a metal platform that shone in the sunlight as though it were brand new. Built upon the metal platform was an oval structure resembling a towering sea wave rushing shore-ward Set into that curving lip was a smooth black oval that glittered like glass.

Bran gestured with his hand. "The well of Molween, acushla."

Peganna shivered. Her hand fell from his and moved to her upper arm, stroking slowly as if to restore its circulation. Cold and suddenly frightened, her eyes seemed held hypnotically by that black opening.

"Bran, suppose it doesn't work?"

"Then we've lost a little time, no more."

His big hand at the small of her back urged her forward. Just so might a supplicant have approached her god ages ago on Earth, with fear etched on her face and in the writhings of her fingers twisting together. Her eyes touched him and fell away. Her lips quivered as she sought to cry a protest and could not.

She stood before the oval on a blue metal band, putting a hand up to her hair, pushing it back. Her lips were a little open.

"What shall I say, Bran?"

"Ask for the perfect weapon."

She nodded, then touched her lips with a tongue-tip "I need a weapon, the perfect weapon," she said slowly. "Give it to me, please."

The black oval glittered, mute.

Peganna uttered a cry of dismay. "Bran, it won't work. It's refused me! After I counted so much on it."

"Don't panic," he told her. "Maybe you didn't ask the right way. Maybe you have to speak in the Crenn Lir tongue. No–that isn't so, if the men who found the well told the truth. They wouldn't have known the language."

"Then what's wrong?"

He said slowly. "The thing may work by some sort of mental

telepathy. Try that. Try picturing a weapon in your mind."

Peganna concentrated. One after another she visualized the weapons of the Lyanir, of the space navies of the Empire. She even thought of handguns and swords, but the black oval remained dead.

She began to sob in her frustration.

"The Crenn Lir had weapons. We know from what we learned of their language and from the paintings we found. Fantastic weapons, some of them, that operated on principles entirely unknown to us. Why doesn't it bring them to me? Why?"

"Maybe it can't, Peganna. They may not exist any more."

Her shoulders slumped as she nodded. "I suppose not. It's been so long—so many centuries. But I felt sure . . . There was a vault that contained all their weapons, sealed away against the ravages of time, which they hoped any who survived the catastrophe could go and open."

Peganna buried her face in her hands, muffling her words. "There must be a way to open that vault—a key of sorts—a word or symbol. . ."

"Keep talking!"

His words were like an electrical stimulation to the woman. Peganna lifted her head, stared with wet eyes at the black oval that was growing lighter, paling to a faint rose. She found herself looking into swirling reds and pinks and lavenders, as if tinted smokes were being blown about by titanic winds, shifting, whirling, driving back and forth, mingling with one another.

". . . a vault of arms, a place where the Crenn Lir could go if any were left alive, to get their weapons, the artifacts of their sciences. There must be a key to that vault—a way to open it! Give me that key. Give the key to me, to Peganna of the Silver Hair. . . ."

A blue egg formed in the oval and moved toward her.

It fell from the oval and bounced across the blue metal dais and rolled to the booted feet of Bran Magannon. He bent down and picked it up.

The reds and pinks and lavenders of the oval blackened swiftly. In an instant it was dark and dead. Peganna gave a sigh and stepped off the dais, staring at the blue egg.

"What is it, Bran?"

"Who knows? A key of some sort, I guess."

His fingers turned it over and over. It was a jewel, they saw when the light struck it, of a crystalline hardness fashioned so that thin red lines ran this way and that inside the blueness. In the hand it was heavy. Cold. Of the size of a chicken egg, it was like nothing Bran the Wanderer had ever seen.

Peganna began to laugh, standing before him with back-thrown head. "We have the key and–we don't know where the lock is that it opens!"

When she grew hysterical between laughter and weeping, Bran drew her into his arms and cradled her head on his chest. He put his words into the thick silver hair that tickled his lips.

"Easy now, mavourneen. There's no need for panic. Somewhere the vault exists. All we have to do is find it."

"Do you know how many planets we'd have to search? Over a thousand! And the vault may be hidden so cleverly that–"

She broke off to weep more fiercely.

Bran said slowly, "For a moment I thought the metal square on Deirdre that hums might be the vault. But there's no place on it in which to put the egg."

"Maybe all we need do is touch it to its surface," Peganna said hopefully, rubbing wet cheeks with the back of her hand.

"I don't think so, but we can try."

Peganna sought to make her voice light, but the undertone of bitter disappointment could not be hidden. "At least we have the key, Bran."

"It isn't much, but it's better than nothing."

He put the blue egg into his belt pouch.

Tiredness was an ache in both of them. They had traveled many worlds through the tele-doors. On some of them it had been day; on some night. Time had become for them only an eternity of movement. Peganna looked pale and drawn, and there were lines at the corners of Bran's eyes.

"We'll stay here a while," he announced.

He found shelter for them in an empty building that once had been a dwelling. Old draperies and furniture were piles of dust now, but Bran built a fire of wood he found beyond the city and made a cozy warmth for them as they slept.

They had no way of knowing how long a day might be on Molween, or how long its nights, but when they woke there was a hushed redness in the air which might have been dawn or dusk. They were very hungry but there was no food to be found on Molween.

Bran lifted Peganna to her feet. "We'll go back to Deirdre," he smiled.

"And test the egg on the humming thing?" she asked. The Wanderer nodded and put his arm about her in reassurance.

The blue egg did nothing to the metal machine when they stood before it once again. Bran touched it to its surface, felt the vibrations through the jewel, but nothing happened. Peganna took her turn, sliding the egg across the metal, holding it high, resting the egg against the metal and walking away.

In despair, she handed it to Bran. "We're getting nowhere. We might as well go home to Miranor. Maybe our scientists have found something in the Crenn Lir writings they're deciphering on Miranor that will give us a clue."

She broke of suddenly and put a hand to her mouth. Above her fingers, her green eyes were wide with dismay. "Oh, I forgot! We have no spaceship! And we can't go back to Makkador for the Crenn Lir ship."

"I have my own ship, Peganna. The one I used before I discovered the tele-doors. It's on one of the Frontier worlds."

The Frontier worlds were planets on the very perimeter of the Empire, lifeless planets for the most part, rich in metals and minerals but unfit for agriculture and with little water. For reasons as yet undetermined by Empire astrologicians, they were to be found close to such shell stars as had been discovered by Empire space explorers. They made excellent hideouts for outlaws and those who grew rich by preying on the merchant ships that plied the space lanes.

There was a tele-door on the planet called Lethe by Empire star mappers, in a small chamber that seemed to have been erected hurriedly by panic-ridden Crenn Lir engineers. Perhaps in the last few hours any of them had to live, as an escape hatch. It was an incomplete building, a desperate searching out for a world on which to flee the mysterious death that hounded down their people.

But the tele-door worked. It had taken Bran the Wanderer out among the Crenn Lir worlds, and now it brought him back. He led Peganna into the Lethean sunlight where his one-man cruiser rested on its vanes.

It was not a large ship; it had been a reject from a consignment ordered by Empire Fleet Command Headquarters nine years before; Bran Magannon had taken advantage of the surplus equipment sales held while he had been a Commander. Ordinarily, no single individual could afford a space ship, except a few multi-billionaire merchants.

"I've never regretted the money it cost," he remarked as Peganna went up the ladder ahead of him. "Without it I couldn't have wandered around the way I did. I'd never have found the tele-doors, either."

He closed the port behind him with a little clang. A quick glance told him the ship was as he had left it, so many months ago. At least the Intergalactic Command troops hadn't seen through one tele-door.

Peganna followed him into the tiny galley, helped him pen sealed cans of meat and pre-cooked vegetables. She put plates and cups on the stilfoam top of a wall folding table ind arranged knives and forks beside them. A sudden thought made her turn toward the open control room door with a smile.

"This will be our second meal together since the Treaty Dinner before you went to Earth from Kuleen," she called.

"Let's hope we have lots more," he replied from the control seat forward. He was adjusting coordinates and relay circuit diodes so that the cybernetic controller could take over the chores of liftoff and shifting into hyperspace gear.

When he was done he threw the starting lever and felt the answering hum sound from beneath the floor-plates. The ionic engine began revving up to takeoff power. Bran came out of the chair. From now on, every move the ship made, until it slowed for a landing on Miranor, would be guided by its own relay circuits.

As they ate, anti-gravitic plates lifted them above Lethe and hurled them outward into space fifty thousand miles. The ship lurched an instant–Bran made a mental note that the hyper-drive gears needed adjustment–then the deep black of space beyond the port windows turned to the misty gray of hyperspace, that universe of no-thing and no-when through which the star-ships traveled.

"A day," he said to Peganna. "No more than at that, surely. Then we'll be on Miranor. I'm going to check my weapons."

"Weapons?" she wondered.

"I'll be frank with you, acushla. I'm thinking about your brother, Gron Dhu. He was mighty friendly with Alvar Drexel eight years ago on Kuleen when we were working out those Treaty details."

Peganna shook her head. "You worry too much. Gron Dhu is Commander of the Lyanir war forces, no more. I'm his sister and his queen. He is bound by custom to obey me."

"Has no one among the Lyanir ever broken a custom, Peganna? Unless I miss my guess, Gron Dhu is an ambitious man."

"Not that ambitious," she stated.

Bran only shrugged and went on eating.

Gron Dhu turned from the window that looked out over the rolling grasslands of the world of Miranor. He was a tall man, heavily muscled through the shoulders that glistened nakedly where the ocana-fur of his military cloak failed to cover them. A dress sword hung in silver chains at his side; when he moved, the chains made faint clanking sounds. His hair was black and closely cropped above a hard brown face. He was a fighting man, and looked it.

He said easily, "You worry too much, Commander Drexel. I have explained it to you, quite thoroughly."

Alvar Drexel gloomed at the tall young Lyanirn from under frowning brows. Necessity and a similarity of ambitions had drawn him to this younger brother of Peganna of the Silver Hair, right from the beginning; as time wore on, he was finding that their destinies were linked even more closely than he had realized.

"You don't know Bran Magannon. He's a devil."

Gron Dhu let his lips thin. "I know Bran Magannon. He and he alone defeated my people. Oh, I remember him, all right. But devil or not, there isn't anything he can do when he and Peganna put themselves in my power by coming back to Miranor. As they will do, sooner or later."

The Empire feet commander shook his head. "The Wanderer always finds a way. It isn't there for you or me to see–but Bran sees it."

The Lyanirn made an impatient gesture. "I've told you what Peganna seeks. A weapon, to use as a wedge to force the Empire to give my people living room. If she finds it, she will bring it here. We capture her–and Bran Magannon–take away the weapon and as ruler of the Lyanir I make peace with the Empire, turning Peganna over to you as a warmonger. If she doesn't find the weapon we're no worse off. She'll come back eventually and when she does, I'll turn her over to you as we've arranged. No matter what, she loses her throne."

"And Bran Magannon his life."

Gron Dhu nodded. He moved away from the window, stepped before a map that took up an entire wall of the large chamber in which he entertained Alvar Drexel. His fingertip touched it, made a circling gesture.

"I've put patrols in the back country, from Wurll to Pandimar. If Peganna tries to avoid us by taking refuge there, my patrols will seize her. But she'll come straight to Andelkrann, which we have made our capitol on Miranor."

"I wish I were as confident as you."

The younger man let his cold black eyes assess his companion. "You had them once, on Makkador. If I'd let them slip from my fingers as you did, perhaps I'd be as worried. You're in a sweat, Commander– which you betrayed by running here to Miranor for my help when Bran and Peganna escaped you on Makkador."

Alvar Drexel half rose from his seat, his face flushed. He sank back soon enough; he was in no position to give free rein to his galled pride. He commented lightly, "Maybe I deserve that, maybe not. I could do no more than give the orders. I could not ride in every zad nor walk with every foot patrol across the planet."

His palm slapped the tabletop with an explosive sound. The golden wine-cup at his elbow trembled. His eyes glowed in feral rage. "A devil! That man's an absolute devil. Always he finds the one way out, the one way to do what must be done!"

"Not this time," snarled Gron Dhu confidently.

The fleet officer brooded at him. "Listen to me. Bran Magannon got off Makkador without a spaceship. Do you understand that? He used no spaceship, yet he left the planet!"

"Maybe he's still there."

Alvar Drexel shook his head. "No, no. He has some other way of traveling. He came to Makkador without a spaceship. He left it the same way. Gods! What I'd give to learn how he did it. Teleportation? Could he have learned its secret during his years among the stars?"

"He won't be able to do his tricks in a prison cell–and we have some fine old dungeons here on Miranor, built eons ago by the Crenn Lir race who called it home." He gestured at the window through which the red ball of a star-sun could be seen. "Were this a younger world, it would suit the Lyanir, but it's old–old. Worn out! Drained of its ancient metals, its chemicals, its loams and vegetation. And bathed by some mysterious force that kills my people unless they swallow medication against its effects."

He swung about, put both palms on the tabletop as he glared down into the upturned face of Alvar Drexel. "Peganna has failed her people, Commander. I shall not fail. You have promised–for my help– that you will see the Lyanir accepted into the Empire."

"As a subject people only," the uniformed man pointed out. "Liable to tribute payments and forced conscriptions. Not as equals. That much, I could not promise."

"The other is enough," Gron Dhu nodded. "From such a beginning, we may hope for more. Peganna was too proud to accept the role of subject people. I'm not–just so long as I'm made rayanor."

He stood with high held head, young and eager, hard and unscrupulous. I was such a youth, mused Commander Drexel, before the years and the disappointments ate so deeply into me. A man does what he may with what talents he possesses. The trouble is, we can boast of so few. So few! Even those we do not learn to control, to use to their best advantage. We can never attain the visions of our inmost selves, never quite create the godlike images we believe ourselves to be. Idols all, with clay feet.

The fleet commander sighed. To be young was to be arrogant of failure, intolerant of anything less than the absolute. Wryly he thought, I hope Gron Dhu has not fashioned his own feet with clay. If Gron Dhu falls, I fall with him. It was not a nice prospect.

Glumly he sipped the tart Molarian wine.

FIVE

THE SHIP came down on Miranor when the dawn was a cool redness on the land, with white wisps of mist rising from the thick clumps of berry bushes and the heat waves dying out across its pale deserts. Below its metal hull men came to stand before their hide tents and stare upward, shielding their eyes from its reflection where sunlight caught it. A thousand feet above the topmost ridges the ship moved, slowly.

Its gray bulk followed the ridges to a winding stream and then slipped out over a stretch of open country. From this flatland they could see the distant spires of a ruined city.

"Andelkrann," murmured Peganna at the port window.

Behind her, Bran turned to a weapon-rack and lifted out thin rods with energy coils about their barrels. Gravely he handed one to her; as gravely, she accepted it, then slipped it into her belt. In exchange she offered him a pill.

"These are as important as the a-guns if you want to stay alive on Miranor," she told him. "Without them, the radiation on the planet will kill you as surely as would an atom beam." Her lips twisted wryly at his scowl, but he swallowed the tablet.

"A planet with a bellyache," he said harshly. "I'm glad I came with you, acushla."

This low over a planet a star-ship needed human hands and so Bran swang back to his control levers, pushing off automatic and guiding the metal hull upward over a rise of rocks. Peganna was at his elbow, standing, pushing back her spill of silver hair.

The land below was old. As there are stars ten billion years old, glowing faintly in their fading heat, as there are young stars with scarcely a million years to their name, so are there young and old planets. Miranor was a planet that knew only its past, having no future as it had no mountains. All the high places had long ago been chipped away by temperature changes and carried off by rain and wind and a glacier here and there. Only the low hills remained, and an occasional ridge to point its crown at the sky.

The little encampments over which they passed were a page torn out of its dim had-been, with the hide huts and the cooking fires set in rings of stones. The men and women wore crude garments for the most part, and the few children Bran saw wore nothing at all. There were bows and arrows on the backs of small bands of hunters over whom they moved, and once Bran caught the flash of a spear-point

It made no sense, Bran told Peganna.

"It makes good sense, if you'll open your mind to it," she told him tartly, fingers digging into his shoulder muscles for emphasis. "Why else do you think I went to Makkador? My people live like nomads because they must. A man needs no atomic energy–which we hoard as zealously as a miser does gold–to put an arrow in a running deer."

Bran grunted and Peganna went on, "The a-guns are stored away in woolen wraps. The women weave garments that are crude and fashionless, but that are also strong and able to stand up to the rigors of a hard existence. When you live in a hide tent, what need is there of silks and satins?"

"Damn the Empire policy makers," he breathed.

"My brother would make submission and trade–in flame pearls and some other knickknacks we've amassed in our travels–for good things and for permission to live here. I say to hell with that!"

Her fire surprised him so that he turned his head and stared up at her. Tears made crystal streaks on her soft cheeks. Then her red mouth curved and her eyes slanted toward his gaze.

"Do I so amaze you, Bran Magannon? Is it so astounding that I want something better for my people than a–than a planet with a bellyache?

I would give them a world with high mountains and tall trees, of grass and water and bushes thick with berries. There the Lyanir would build cities that could compete in beauty with your own."

"You don't have to argue with me," he said.

"I only explain the tents and arrows, darling. We hoard our treasures, being a sensible people. We put away the a-guns and the silken garments until we can use and wear them properly."

A maze of stone and marble lifted into view along the horizon. Andelkrann, Peganna whispered again, bending to stare at the ancient ruin. As they neared its spires and fluted columns, Bran saw that beyond it, row on row until they made a metal forest, were the gray metal hulls of the Lyanirn spaceships. Put away in mothballs, in a manner of speaking, against the moment of their need.

On two of the nearer ships there was movement as ray-barrels in their gun mounts swung to cover their progress. At any moment those weapons might spit red destruction at his little ship, Bran knew, and shivered to the coldness at his spine.

The guns menaced, but they did not speak.

He set his star-ship down in an open space between the ships and the city itself. Peganna was running to the hatch controls before the engines stilled, unhooking the locks and swinging wide the door. Cool air came into the compartment as she stood poised there in the opening, a white arm lifted.

At sight of her the people ran forward. Eager hands lifted to catch and hold her as she descended the ladder. They love her, Bran thought, following her to the ground. See how they crowd about, touching her almost reverently, laughing in delight at her safe return.

From their queen, the people looked at Bran Magannon.

Some of them remembered him from the treaty planet, Kuleen. A few eyes opened wide and tongues wagged, but mostly they were indifferent to his presence. Peganna had brought him here; he would be respected as her guest, despite the fact that they owed their present misery in large part to this man.

Peganna turned and held out her hand to him. He caught it, pressed it, then walked beside her like a brazen giant in fur kilt and leather jacket, a-gun bumping to his stride at a hip. Where her shadow touched the ground, his was also, like a protecting spirit.

At one time in some remote past, Andelkrann had been a mighty metropolis. It stretched for miles, all white marble and tile rooftops, stone edifices massive above more dainty temples and long porticoes. Its streets were flagged in the same hardness that Bran had seen on other Crenn Lir worlds. Fountains splashed their waters–pure now after the unknown millennia that had passed since the Crenn Lir had died out–the great statues in stone and some red metal told onlookers that the Crenn Lir had been a handsome race.

Bran might have paused to study the statues more closely, but the soft hand in his tugged him on, almost at a trot. The green eyes that laughed at him and the pretty red mouth urging him to greater speed would hear of no delay. Now that they were on Miranor, Peganna was impatient to test the blue egg.

Two warriors at a gateway saluted their queen.

A door swung open and they moved inside, to a garden. Only a few hardy plants bloomed here, relics of the Lyanir past on their home world, transplanted now but scarcely thriving. Past all these the girl brought him, with a lightness to her step that told the man how happy she was at her homecoming.

The darkness of a corridor beckoned. They went through it into a room so massive they felt dwarfed. The furniture which had been carried from the star-ships seemed lost in this magnificence of faded wall murals and paving-stone floor.

Bran turned when he saw a shadow.

He was too late. A hand clamped on his gun wrist and a brawny forearm hooked his throat. From the corner of an eye he saw two men gripping Peganna, a hairy hand stiffing her scream as she was swung up off her feet and held helpless. A red fury took hold of Bran at sight of her being manhandled, so that he cursed the men who held him.

He went limp and fell. His weight tugged the men off balance. As his knees touched the floor his body erupted sideways. He hit the men who had been clutching him and sent them flying with a rolling body block. His right hand went to his holstered a-gun.

The men died there in its blast, eyes wide.

He swung toward Peganna but he could not fire for fear of hitting her. The beam from an a-gun is needle-thin but the Lyanirn were moving this way and that as they dragged the girl backward, and her legs kicking out in futile anger blocked his aim.

More warriors were moving in, now. They held no a-guns, only stunners. Bran guessed that their orders were to take him alive. Their bluish beams came at him from all angles.

Where those beams hit, they packed the wallop of a mule. One had only to touch him in his head to knock him senseless, and so he darted sideways, throwing himself fat then rolling to avoid them. One hit a thigh and almost paralyzed a leg. Another caught his left arm and numbed it.

He fired back until the a-gun stank. Some he hit, killing them instantly; others he missed, bringing down marble powder from the walls. It was sacrilege to fight in such a place as this, he thought fleetingly, knowing what an Earth archaeologist would give to stand here and study those murals, but his life and that of Peganna of the Silver Hair were at stake.

The blows he took from the stun-beams affected his animal speed. He slowed just enough that the others could bring their weapons to a focus. He caught three bolts on his chest that rammed him into a marble column. He took another in the left thigh and something hit his gun-wrist, almost breaking it. It was as though he had been hammered against the wall by psychic spears. His body shuddered as blue beam after blue beam hit his middle, his chest, his shoulders.

Enough of these blows, and his body would be pulp. It was like having horses kick a man to death. Blood was running from his nostrils under the repeated hammerings. The Lyanir had him spreadeagled and helpless, and they were going to make him suffer before they gave him the mercy of unconsciousness.

A girl was screaming, somewhere. Peganna?

Bran shook his head. It did no good. He was slipping down the wall, legs gone out from under him. Human muscle would accept only so much. He collapsed and his vision blurred.

He lay there inert, forgotten.

Yet his ears were alive, so that he heard the voice of Gron Dhu as he spoke with his sister. Triumph lay in his tones, and arrogance.

". . . queen no longer, Peganna! Instead, I take over the role of the Lyanir. Where you have always failed, I shall succeed. Commander Drexel!"

Boot-steps approached. There was a slight pause, as though a man bowed.

"Tell her!"

"It is so, highness. Your brother and I have come to terms. I shall make application for admission to the Empire for your people."

"As equals?" There were tears in her voice, Bran thought as he lay supine, poised between the utter blackness of oblivion and this dreaming state where he lived only in a realm of sound. Well, she had seen what they had done to him.

"As equals–no. I'm afraid not. But as friends, yes. Required only to pay a token tribute in submission, required–"

"–to be slaves! Is this your great success, brother?"

There was the sound of a blow and Bran stirred deep inside him with a searing fury. Gron Dhu rasped, "Take her away. To the tower. The other–to the cells below. I'll give out word a little later that Bran Magannon killed the queen and that he has paid for his murder with his life."

Feet shuffled. Then Gron Dhu said, "No–wait."

A hand fumbled and Peganna cried out. Gron Dhu asked softly, "This blue egg you carry, sister mine–what is it? Oh, I can tell from your face it's priceless enough. But–how? And why?"

She made no answer. In a moment there was the sound of another blow. Bran the Wanderer stirred physically now, moving in a spasmodic shudder on the floor flaggings. His great hands opened and closed.

"You will talk. There are ways of making a woman speak. Or a man. Suppose I were to work you over with the stunners. How long would Bran Magannon remain silent?"

"You filthy devil!"

"Ah, it touches you, does it? Good. Then perhaps, if you possess the sense I think you do, you'll tell me what I want to know."

There was no sound for a little while and it was as if Bran Magannon had died. Then hands touched him, lifting him, held him upright.

"A pretty sight, your handsome ex-commander. Blood all over him, his flesh raw. I don't even know if he's alive."

"Bran, Bran . . . ohhh, Subb of the Hundred Hates!"

"Weep, dear sister. It will make it easier for you to watch as we ruin him as a man before your eyes."

The Wanderer tried to gather himself to break free, but there was no strength left anywhere in his body. Only the hands at his arms and armpits held him upright. He was a rag doll, with just about as much stuffing inside him. Yet he knew that even in his dark world, agony so intense as to be blinding would come to him if Gron Dhu did what he threatened.

Peganna understood it, too.

"I yield. The egg will open a secret vault on Miranor, or so I think." She went on speaking of how she and Bran had gone to the well of Molween and how she had made her wish. The blue egg had been her gift from the well, from the dead race of Crenn Lir. "I think it's some sort of key, a key to a vault in which the Crenn Lir left their weapons and their scientific artifacts."

When she was done speaking, a man sighed.

"It could be," murmured Alvar Drexel. "Though where the vault is— who can say? It might be anywhere in space."

"We Lyanir have deciphered many of the Crenn Lir writings," Gron Dhu said excitedly. "By Lur! I'll have every man-jack scientist working night and day to find something about this thing, or about the vault it opens."

"If there is a vault," the Earthman said heavily, looking at Peganna. Gron Dhu intercepted his glance and smiled wickedly.

"I know my sister. I can tell when she lies and when she speaks the truth. She honestly believes the egg is a key. And–so do I."

The arms that held Bran lifted him a little higher and began to move him. All he could hear now was the pad of military boots on the floor flaggings and a sound of breathing. After a while, even that went away.

Then he was truly dead to the world about him.

Time is finite. It moves while a man lies in an eternity of nothingness. Time moves and time gleams with light as a lamp touches the stone walls of a cell where a man lies locked in rusted manacles. In the glare of the lamp a platter with food is lowered to the floor.

Hands lifted the man and a metal container touched his lips. Some of the liquid in the container dribbled from his lips but enough trickled down his throat so that after a while he stirred and opened his eyes.

The light blinded him. "Eat," said a voice.

The lamp went away and he was in darkness again but now his senses were alive and though the pain in his big body made him shudder, he was well enough and hungry enough to crawl to the platter and wolf down the food it held. The metal bottle was close at hand, too. He upended it and drank its contents slowly.

It was a form of wine that had been treated medicinally, quite obviously. It was cool and soothing to the throat and after a short time he seemed to feel its potency working in his veins.

Bran lay back on the cold stone and made a pillow of his arms where he bent them under his neck. He wanted to think but his eyelids were heavy and so he slept. When he woke he felt refreshed, and the light was in his eyes again. A second platter of food was here and this time there was more food than before, so that when he was done eating, some of his old strength was in his muscles.

Three more times the lamp came with food and drink. Bran did not sleep so much now, and he exercised as he could, walking back and forth the length of his chains. He thought of hitting the man who came with the lamp but the jailer knew to a nicety how far his chains would stretch and he always put the platters down where Bran could reach them but not him.

Why are they keeping me alive?

The question burned in his brain during the hours when he lay alone in the blackness of the cell. Perhaps Peganna had made some sort of bargain with her brother. Let Bran Magannon live and Peganna would support her brother in his usurpation of her throne. She would have done it, he realized, if she were given the chance.

Yet Gron Dhu did not need his sister.

His lie that Bran the Wanderer–who had driven them out of habitable space to this dead planet!–had murdered Peganna, would be believed. The people of Miranor would have no reason to doubt it.

His fingers curled into talons with the desire to lock about the throat of Gron Dhu. No, her brother could kill Peganna and Bran Magannon and no one would ever know it. Why then was he keeping him alive?

And for how long?

The answer to that came the next time his jailer brought him food and drink. The wine in the metal bottle was drugged. He knew this a few minutes after he had eaten and finished the wine. He had just waked from a deep slumber yet now he found himself sinking back into sleep. He tried to fight the inertia that gripped him, but could not.

When he opened his eyes, there was a lamp burning on a wooden table not ten feet away. A radium lamp, he guessed, of the sort he had seen in the possession of the Lyanir on Kuleen. He stood up and there was no clank of rusted metal. His chains were gone and the manacles with them that had held his wrists and ankles.

Bran the Wanderer was a realist.

Gron Dhu was not making his life any easier. There was a reason for this pseudo-freedom. It was a refinement of cruelty, he felt positive, and like a wild animal in a trap, he waited for what was to happen.

The answer came in a feral scream.

A man shouted curses beyond the bolted door to his prison cell and there was a sound of wheels moving. Again the cry raised the hairs at the nape of his neck. This was a wild animal screaming in mad fury, a cat of some sort with sharp fangs and rending claws. They were dragging its cage along the corridor.

Bran looked around him helplessly, knowing there was no weapon to be found yet aware of a desperate need to stay alive. He was strong now, healthy; not the near-dead thing that had been carried into this prison. A chuckle rasped his throat. Gron Dhu was a clever man. He wanted Bran Magannon to suffer, and so he had let him recover from the stunners, had let his body heal and grow strong so it would be a long time dying.

The manacles had been knocked away for the same reason. Gron Dhu wanted him able to fight for his life, yet to feel it slipping slowly and then more slowly from him as he battled the cat. This was the reason for the lamp, as well: so he could see the manner of his dying.

The door was opening. Bran tensed.

Could he make a run for it? Slip past the animal in some fashion and ram into the guards who were behind it? No. The cage had been wheeled to the doorway and one side lifted up so that as the door opened the cat could move only into the cell.

The lamp on the table showed the cat, a big spotted korst. It was not a native of Miranor but then Miranor had no native animal life any more. Even the deer and the sheep that grazed on its slopes and in its sparse forests had been brought here by the Lyanir and allowed to run wild.

The korst sighted Bran. Its head lowered and its green eyes stared with unwinking steadiness. Beyond it was a lighted corridor and the bars of its cage. Through them Bran caught a glimpse of grinning guards, crowding forward to watch the fun.

A snarl formed in the thickly furred throat of the big cat. It padded forward, easily. Bran watched it, putting a hand on the tabletop. He had no chance against the korst. It was too big, too strong. One rake of its hind claws could disembowel him. One bite of its white fangs could take away his face.

Heat burned his fingers where he had put them about the base of the lamp. Slowly he let his fingers tighten, trying to ignore the pain to get a grip on the metal base. There was molten metal inside the lamp, treated with radium. It would last an indefinite time, used as a lamp.

Used as a weapon–

His hand lifted and the lamp came with it, hurled across the cell in a side-wise throwing motion of his arm. His action had been so swift the korst did not realize what was happening until the lamp hit it full in the face. The lamp broke, its radioactive metal spilling across the mouth and jaw of the beast.

The korst screamed and leaped.

Bran was not there to meet its claws. He was racing through the sudden darkness of the cell to the door, slamming it shut. Faintly he could hear the outcries of the guards, balked of their fun. He crouched on widespread feet, waiting for what he would see.

The cell was dark, now. The molten liquid was a pool of blackness on the floor. The only light was that which came from cracks in the cell door. It was enough.

Bran could see the eyes of the cat glittering like green diamonds lit by inner fires. He knew where the beast was, at any rate. There was not enough light for the korst to see him, at least not plainly. If he moved silently and without too quick a motion, he might find a way to win this fight.

He inched across the floor on careful feet. One advantage was his, one alone. He knew the layout of the chamber, its little recesses. The korst was in a strange lair and in the manner of cats all over the stars, it waited with patience until it could learn where it was.

There was no time for that.

He was close to the beast, here by the table. Normally the cat would have smelled him but the dank foulness of the cell was all about it, smothering the keenness of its nostrils. Gently Bran grasped a table leg. It was metal and cold to his touch. Metal leg, wooden top. He knew that much at least, from what his eyes had told him before he had sung the lamp.

His muscles tensed as he yanked.

The korst screamed and whirled. The metal leg held but he got the table up and heard claws rip splinters from its top. The korst was not used to fighting on its hind legs. It screeched in fury and fell back to all fours.

Bran wrenched again at the table leg, hearing wood give.

Five times he tugged before the screws tore and the leg came away. He wondered why the guards did not open the door, but he was grateful for their restraint.

His eyes hunted through the blackness.

Yes–there were the beast's green diamond eyes.

Bending, he slipped off his sandals and advanced on bare toes. The metal leg was a long club in his right hand. The blazing eyes turned toward him. Bran leaped. He struck down hard with the leg and in the instant of impact, leaped sideways away from the paw that was sure to rake at him.

The korst was screaming thickly, again and again. The eyes were gone, then reappeared across the room. They darted this way and that before Bran realized that the cat was racing back and forth across the cell in a savage, desperate hunt for the man who had wounded it.

On bare feet, the Wanderer moved against the wall. He did not want to be pinned here by some wild rush, by a lucky swing of claws. The eyes were still, suddenly.

Bran swung. The cat coughed and rose up. Full in its face Bran swung his metal club, with both hands tight about the handle. The jar of the blow sent shock into his muscles but the cat fell away. He heard a thump.

Bran waited, rigid. If the cat were unconscious and its eyes closed, he would have to hunt for it with his hands. He moved, his toe touching warm fur. In panic, Bran struck.

Again and again he brought that club down on the body before him. He never knew how long he might have stood there, striking. When his body was wet with sweat and he stood in little pools of what must be blood, he let the air whistle through his lips and stood to his full height.

The cat was dead. Bran cried out and fell face down.

He had put all his ability into that single scream. He cut it off suddenly and hoped the guards had heard it and were convinced of its authenticity. He lay with his face partly turned toward where he thought the door might be. He waited.

After a time the door opened slightly. A rectangle of yellow light came into the cell and touched the korst. Bran heard a man call out in amazement. The yellow rectangle widened into a square as the door opened even further.

"He killed it," the guard said to himself. "He actually killed that thing before it killed him too."

There was blood all over him, Bran knew, but it was the blood of the korst. In the light from the corridor, it looked as if he had been clawed to death. Footfalls sounded behind him. A hand touched his shoulder to roll him over.

Bran struck with his rock-like fist.

The guard grunted and collapsed on him. Over his motionless body, the Wanderer stared at the lighted corridor. Thank Kronn! There was just this one guard to account for. For the moment, anyhow.

Bran rolled him over, fumbled at his belt.

His fingers closed on a stunner. It was no a-gun but it was a lot better weapon than the table-leg. He tugged it free of the guard's belt and moved to the door and into the corridor. Carefully he closed and bolted the cell door behind him. The cage had been pushed to one side, evidently until the guard found out if the korst was still alive.

He was free to try and find Peganna.

Still in his bare feet, his boots behind him in the cell, he raced down the corridor. Voices raised in the low hum of casual talk made him leap into a recess. More warriors? Yes, but they were not coming along the corridor. They were in a small room that served as a guardhouse.

He would have to pass them all to get out of the prison.

And yet–perhaps not! This recess where he stood was part of a doorway. His fingers fumbled until they found a stud. Pressing it, he was relieved to hear the door slid back on tiny bearings. Another corridor lay in front of him.

This tunnel lead to another and then to a third. After ten minutes he was hopelessly lost in this maze of subterranean passages. One thing alone he noticed as he walked. He was moving slowly toward something that throbbed more loudly at each step he took. Curiosity caught him in its grip. He had to see the thing that made this rhythmic sound which by now was shaking the stone on which he placed his feet.

A door opened to his touch and he found himself staring in at a small nuclear reactor. Surprise held him rigid. A reactor, here? In the depths of the old Crenn Lir city of Andelkrann? It was not possible. Then common sense caught hold of him. The reactor had not belonged to the Crenn Lir. It was the property of the Lyanir.

The big city would be difficult to heat, at best. The Lyanir would have to have some way of making their lives as comfortable as possible. This motor was their answer to the problem. It would feed heat and perhaps coolness during the worst days of summer, to the rooms of the inhabited section of the city.

He was turning away when a thought struck him.

On bare feet he padded down into the huge chamber that housed the motor. What he needed might be here, but he must go carefully, the stunner in his hand ready to hit and hit hard should he be discovered.

A nuclear reactor needs little attention, once it has been set to functioning. For hours at a time it would be left to itself. Yet being a machine, there would be things to go wrong with it. Bran hunted for what must be down here, a manual of some sort that would tell when and where to look for trouble.

And with it, a floor plan of the house fed by the reactor. His eyes hunted for a desk, a cubbyhole of sorts. He found it in the shadows of a heat exchanger, a little table covered with papers.

He went through them carefully before he found what he needed, and spread out the map on the tabletop. Scanning its diagrams, he began from the heart of the maze, the reactor chamber, and worked outward. Though he spoke the Lyanir tongue, he was confused by the written language; yet he could understand enough to locate the great tower in which Gron Dhu had placed Peganna.

He began to memorize the tunnels and the stairs he would have to cross before he stood in the tower itself. There was a wall chronometer near one of the doorways which showed the hour of dusk. Bran tried to think back, to remember what he had learned of Lyanir custom during the weeks he had been on Kuleen. Soon after dusk, the dining tables would be groaning with food, yes. And Gron Dhu with Alvar Drexel, if he were still here, would be at one of those tables.

Bran checked his stun gun, then moved out.

Only one person touched his vision on the ramp to the upper floors, a man with the ornate double-ax on his jerkin that showed him for an officer. Bran hit him in the head with the stunner and left him unconscious. The man had been downed from behind; he might never learn who had done it, nor who had stripped him of his uniform.

There was more danger on the main floor, since there were more people moving about on their tasks. Bran hugged shadows for a little time, then decided to trust in the stolen uniform he wore. He walked easily, unhurriedly. Nobody even glanced at him.

He was up three fights of marble stairs and at the great oak door–a new one, since the old had powdered long centuries ago–before there was trouble. The guard left at the tower entrance saluted crisply and maintained his wooden face while he told Bran no one was permitted beyond this point.

There was no avoiding it. Bran hit him with his fist, a side-wise blow that traveled six inches, no more. It drove the man's head halfway around on his shoulders and banged him into the oak door, where Bran pinned him with a hand lest he betray what had happened by falling.

There was a key to the door. Was it on the belt of the man with his back to the planks and his head lolling so loosely? No, by Lur! It was somewhere else. There was no desk here with a drawer. Nor was there a peg with a key-ring hanging from it.

Sweat touched the Wanderer as he stood there holding up a senseless man. To have come so far and–now to fail! Desperately his eyes searched. Nothing! He was tempted to use his stun-gun on the lock to see if he might jar it loose.

The solution to his problem made him chuckle.

He lifted his fist and knocked. There was movement on the other side of the door. "Open up inside," he said crisply.

A key turned. The door opened. Bran shot from the hip right into the middle of the man staring at him on the other side of the doorway. The stunner had the kick of a mule. The man went down in a heap.

Bran propped up the outside guard as best he could, to simulate a man on duty. Then he pushed the other man out with him and locked the door from the inside.

He took the winding staircase three steps at a time, confident there were no more guards. Nor were there. The door to the tower rooms pushed open to the fat of his palm on its wood.

Peganna was sitting at a window, staring out at the moon-drenched land. Her shoulders were rounded, her hair loose and unkempt, as though she did not care how she might look. Hands on fist, Bran surveyed her.

"A fine figure of a girl in love, I must say!"

Her head swiveled and her eyes grew enormous. Her lips opened, quivered uncontrollably. She started to tremble.

Bran held out his arms.

She flew to him, was crushed and held tight for long minutes. When he let her go she was laughing through her tears. "Was there ever a man like you? How in the name of Lur did you do it?"

"It was my luck, mavourneen. And the good use I make of the brain God gave me. Is there any way out of this place except the way I came up?"

"I'm afraid not."

"Hmmm. It will be awkward." He scowled and, putting her aside gently, went to stand at the window. Below him in the moonlight was the city of Andelkrann, half in ruins, half with the touch of fires in its buildings, where women cooked and feasted with their men. It was a far drop to the pavements below, even to the nearest roof.

On the opposite wall was a second window. Fifty feet below and ten feet across with a gap between the walls was a roof with a long pitch to it where a man might stand without fear of falling backward. Bran studied it, then turned to look around the room.

There was a couch and a small table with a chair. No bed-sheets to tear into strips, no rug to the stone floor to shred and make into rope. Bran sighed and removed the jacket of his stolen uniform.

"There's no help for it, Peganna. This will never form a long enough rope but we've got to make the try." His strong hands tore the jacket in half. He knotted the sleeves together and slipped out of the trousers.

He wore his fur kilt and leather jerkin, now. The jerkin he removed and began to tear into strips. The woman watched him almost breathlessly, looking from the window to his working hands. Suddenly her lips tightened and she bent to rip the hem of the gown she was wearing.

"No," protested Bran, "there's no need for you to ruin your pretty clothes. We'll make enough of a thing to hang from with what I have."

"That 'thing' won't reach fifty feet and you know it, Bran Magannon. Now be still and–here! Give me a hand with this where the seam is sewn."

The gold brocade ripped to the tug of his fingers. To her upper thighs he tore it, then shredded it across. His eyes touched her legs a moment as he grinned, "You have fine legs, acushla."

"Keep your mind on the rope, Bran Magannon."

"I'm only thinking that you'll be able to run faster now," he told her and laughed as she swung a palm at him.

When the rope was finally knotted together, it was pitifully short. Even Bran looked dubious, though he carried it to the window and fastened one end to a chair-leg, propping the chair side-wise to the wall across the window.

Gingerly he crawled through the window, holding the rope which he played down along the side of the tower wall. Peganna was watching him with wide eyes, hands lifted to her long silver hair, twisting it up and about her head in a topknot.

"Peganna darling," he said worriedly, looking down.

"Hold your tongue, Bran. Remember–you belong to me."

"Why, so I do. I'd forgotten the little dice game we had."

"Then give me your hand and hold the rope."

She put a leg over the sill and rested a foot on his shoulder. Gently she slid out, sliding down his back, locking her legs to his thighs and clinging to his chest with her arms.

"Am I heavy?"

"Save your breath," he growled.

Hand over hand Bran went down the makeshift rope until its end was a scant three inches from his fingers where he had tied a knot to prevent their sliding off.

He looked below him. The roof was close to fifty feet down and ten feet across, above a long fall to death on the ancient cobblestones. He drew a deep breath.

"I'm going to swing you out, acushla–and drop you."

"Do it fast. Fast–so I can't think!"

She let his right hand take her wrists and hold them. He lowered her slowly, while the muscles of the hand and arm that held the rope knotted with convulsive strength. Back and forth he swung her, like a pendulum. Moonlight touched her upturned face with its heights of silver hair and Bran felt his heart lurch into his throat at sight of her.

"If you miss, I'll follow you down," he whispered.

Her eyes opened to stare up, bravely.

He said, though it cost him needed energy, "I couldn't stand to be without you again, mavourneen."

She smiled and as she smiled, he let her go, at the end of her swing with her feet pointing at a tangent to the wall. She dropped like an arrow and Bran knew an instant of stark terror when it seemed he had not properly calculated the distance. Then her feet touched the rooftops and her legs crumpled and she sprawled full length on the tiles.

Bran closed his eyes, then opened them.

It was a simple matter for him to grip the rope with both hands, to prop his feet against the wall and use it as a springboard to propel him more than a dozen feet straight out so that when he fell he landed a little beyond Peganna.

He whirled and caught her, kissing her.

Overhead the lone moon of Miranor turned endlessly about its parent planet, its silver beams made a pallid fire of her hair as Peganna clung to him, shaking uncontrollably.

"I was so afraid, so afraid."

"No more than I was myself."

She nestled against him. "Just hold me for a little time, Bran. Until my heart slows down."

It was foolish to kneel here holding the girl he loved for all her world to see them, but the perfume of her hair and the taste of her kisses on his lips made Bran the Wanderer a man without a worry. He let her go when he felt her fumbling at his belt-pouch.

"Here," she said, holding out two pills.

Bran laughed. He caught Peganna and held her while mirth convulsed him in its grip. After what they had been through, those two pills against the radiation still on Miranor were anti-climactic.

"I put them in your pouch because I knew you'd never think to take them otherwise," she told him, glee shining in her green eyes. "Now go on. Swallow one."

He did as she ordered, then lifted her to her feet.

They were still far from safety, but they were in the open and there would be a way off this roof to the streets. In the streets there were shadows where a man and woman might hide as they ran.

SIX

DAWN FOUND them on the outskirts of the city, crossing a great square. Bran walked with the stunner in his fist and Peganna a step behind at his elbow. His luck had held through the night, all the way from the tower. There had been few travelers in the dark-time hours, and those few they had avoided easily enough by hiding when they approached.

When the open country stretched before them, Bran halted.

"Where do we go now, mavourneen?"

"Into the hills, to the hide tents of my *dravi*."

The *dravi* was her clan, Peganna explained. The clan was the foundation on which the entire structure of the Lyanir was based. A dozen clans made up a *dravi*, and there were fifty *dravi* in the entire nation. Upwards of ten thousand men, women and children comprised a single *dravi*, united by the loyalties that had come down from the days when the Lyanir had hunted with stone axes.

"We will be safe there. Gron Dhu won't dare risk the anger of the clan chief. It's a form of sanctuary."

Bran was dubious but could think of no alternative. Gron Dhu would dare anything to get what he wanted, even if it meant stamping out an entire clan. His only hope was that the warriors needed for such a task might refuse to obey his order.

His hand caught her fingers, but as he went to step out across the grasses, she held him back, telling him she had enough exercise for one day. There would be air-sleds in the buildings on the rim of the city, that were used by royal messengers in a hurry.

"I am still queen of the Lyanir," she informed him proudly. "Those air-sleds belong to me."

Bran grunted but went where she walked. He was surprised there had been no alarm, no search parties out for them. When he mentioned this to Peganna, she laughed harshly.

"Gron Dhu is locked away with the scientists, examining the blue egg. They have been making tests of it for the past six days. Gron Dhu is highly excited. He is as confident as I am myself the egg will open a vault. It gives off a type of radiation that might unlock a door, once it's fitted into its cradle. He has no time for you and me, darling–not yet, at least."

"And Alvar Drexel?"

"Gone back to Earth to offer its politicians a fortune in flame pearls to let the Lyanir submit to Earth empire as one of its conquered peoples." Bitterness tinged her throat as she said, "Gron Dhu will make a fine rayanor! Already he has sold his people into slavery."

They moved silently through the red dawn.

The air-sleds were lengths of highly polished wood and metal that reminded Bran of big surfboards. Twenty feet long and between three and six feet wide, depending on whether they were to carry one or two passengers, each was fitted with a miniature motor and eight small jets protruding from its stern. They were so light to handle, Peganna was able to slide one forward on its four retractable wheels, then lie face down behind the transparent wind canopy.

She explained the controls to Bran as he strapped her down. "This lever is for speed. This is for elevation. This is for maneuverability. Any questions?"

He laughed and slapped her rump.

"I could fly this stick in my sleep. Get on with you. III come after directly."

He waited until she was airborne, then strapped himself on his own sled and shifted its three sticks. The sled rolled easily across the ground, lifted with a whine of air tearing through its vents. The canopy protected the flier from the rush of air, though there was a breathing mask attached to a tank of oxygen beside the controls. It did not make for a comfortable ride it a man were nervous by nature, but it was a smooth one.

Ten minutes after he was aloft, Bran realized he was enjoying himself. The sled was a splinter under him so that the only sensation he could liken it to was actual flying. He could spiral into a dive and pull out. He could stand on his tail and go straight up. He could parallel the ground at a speed that was governed only by his ability to breathe the air through which he raced. For fast couriers, there was the oxygen mask.

Yet he and Peganna made good enough time, even without the masks. They slipped like bullets above a world where the vegetation was stunted and lacked vitality, where the trees were small, where water was a problem since the oceans had long ago dried up and only the lakes and mountain brooks survived, fed as they had been for millennia by underground streams.

In the distance trees made a green carpet over the low, rounded hills and a blue haze above a valley showed where grasses grew between gaunt rocks. Except for the invisible radiation that was everywhere, this might still be a pleasant world on which to live. The pills which the Lyanir were forced to take made it intolerable, Bran knew. The pills gave them life but it was a form of slavery against which their proud spirits rebelled.

Ahead of him Peganna swerved her sled. Obediently he followed, to watch the ground change below them into a series of rocky uplifts sloping toward higher ground. The terrain was different now. Gone were the meadows and the fields of grass, for the timber line was below and trees bent by the wind, and thick layers of moss, went on without end, up into the regions where a cold morass of towering groundsel took over.

Peganna pointed.

Bran could see hide tents sprawling across a level where yellow moss lay like a carpet and tall heathers rose upward toward the clouds. A hunting party drew back as they darted overhead. A woman filling a jar with water from a mountain stream paused to wave.

Then they were lowering ground-ward, flashing above the yellow moss at a height of ten feet, five and lower. Sled wheels scraped and bounced as the fliers swayed to a halt.

The tents seemed deserted. Peganna swung off the sled and stretched, staring around her. When Bran came to stand at her side, she frowned.

"Where are the people?" she asked.

There was an utter stillness in the air. Then there was a clang of metal on metal and the roar of excited voices. Peganna whirled and ran, with Bran beside her. Where the rock slope dropped away to a mossy amphitheatre, the clan clustered in a great circle about two men.

The men faced one another with shields on their left arms and swords in their hands. One man was old, with gray in his hair and in the beard that moved where the wind caught it; the other was young, with a deep chest and long arms. He held his shield low, looking over its rim at the older man.

"Give way, Parkan," he called. "There's no disgrace to step down from the chieftainship."

"Only when you prove you can fell me, Avrak!"

Peganna shivered and drew closer to Bran who put an arm about her middle. She whispered, "It was so in the old days, before we left Lyanol. I had thought the old ways forgotten but I see they were only suspended in our long trip across space. The clan may get a new chief this afternoon."

The younger man was attacking, swinging his blade in great slashes that dug deep cuts in the shield that held him off. Bran watched with an almost professional interest, having fenced on more than one Space

Fleet team for the honor of representing the Service at an Olympiad. He was a stranger to the shield, though, and found himself fascinated by the ease with which Parkan swung his about to intercept the rain of blows that came at him from all directions.

"They call this duel the *dravi-kor*," Peganna said. "It has been a part of our culture for endless generations. The winner need not kill the other. A blow on the head to knock him out would be sufficient. I think this is what young Avrak intends, since Parkan is his uncle."

Bran watched the play of the swords, finding his blood pounding faster in his veins. There was something elemental in this struggle for mastery of the clan. It had its roots deep in the ancient cultures of man wherever he existed, wherever he had risen out of savagery into civilization. Just so might men have fought on Earth with stone axes, with stabbing swords, with claymores, though there had been no formal rite to it as there was among the Lyanir, and the custom had long since faded into oblivion with the duel.

He glanced sideways at Peganna, "And the rayanal? Is she also subject to the *dravi-kor*?"

She smiled faintly. "Yes, except that we call it the *raya-kor*. The queen does not fight herself, naturally. Her champion fights for her."

"Who is your champion?"

She smiled wryly. "My brother, Gron Dhu. He has a great reputation with the sword and shield, has Gron Dhu. He made my reign safe except when he began to know ambition."

Below them, the old man was tiring. His shield moved slower and slower. Avrak forced the fighting, swift in his movements and untiring. He put his blade against his uncle and wove a web of steel around him until Parkan stood panting with weariness.

Then Avrak leaped. His blade rose and fell. The flat of it took Parkan alongside the head and the old man fell like a tree going down in a gale.

Bending, Avrak tore loose the gold band on his uncle's arm and put it on his own. The sunlight caught it, made it shimmer as Avrak tossed his shield and sword aside and bent above the fallen man. They could hear him calling for water and bandages and healing herbs.

Peganna sighed and stirred. "It's like a symbol or–an omen. Am I to lose my queenship as Parkan lost his chieftainship, of a sword-stroke? Or–have I already lost it?"

Bran made no answer.

They walked down the rocky slope and among the people who drew back at first and then rushed forward with glad cries, surrounding Peganna in pleasure and delight. As she had been greeted at Andelkrann, before Gron Dhu had captured her, so now she was greeted, patted and kissed by the women, admired and bowed to by the men.

Leaving his uncle to the hands of his womenfolk, Avrak came forward to meet his rayanal. He would have gone down on a knee except that Peganna caught his hands and held them.

"I may no longer be your queen, Avrak," she smiled, and went on to speak of how Gron Dhu had treated her in Andelkrann.

The new chief shook his reddish hair. "No man rules the Lyanir while you live, Peganna." He looked pleased as a shout went up at his words. His new role sat his shoulders like an ill-made cloak, Bran thought, but in time it would smooth to a good fit.

Parkan was coming forward, head wrapped in a white cloth, leaning his weight on the shoulder of a grandson. He stood beside Avrak and listened while Peganna explained why she had gone to Makkador and what had befallen her after she had met with Bran Magannon.

It was night when she was done talking, seated on a little stool beside Avrak, staring down into the fires where the evening meal was cooking. Bran sat cross-legged to one side of her. Old Parkan was just beyond Avrak, sipping occasionally from a cup that held wine with crushed herbs in it. The old man had accepted the new chief cheerfully enough; privately, Bran thought he was rather pleased at the outcome. He had been chief for close to half a century; let another hold the office and know its cares! Yet he was determined to add his voice to the advice that would pepper Avrak for a time, until he had enough confidence in his judgment to make his own decisions.

Peganna said, "The blue egg is the key, we hope. All we have to find is the lock it fits."

Avrak growled, "And Gron Dhu? Will he come seeking you here?"

"If he does, what will you do?" Bran wondered.

"If he threatens my queen, I'll fight," Avrak said simply.

"Against the whole nation?"

Parkan leaned forward, watching Avrak. What he saw in his hard face seemed to satisfy him, for he buried his mouth in his wine-cup

"To the last man, the last woman, if need be. The clan of the Ax swore allegiance to Peganna. While she lives the oath is binding."

"Let me release you, Avrak," Peganna said sweetly.

The young chief shook his head. "Only death can do that, highness. Yours or mine." He grinned suddenly. "And we're both too young to think of the grave."

Bran leaned forward, saying, "Number me among your warriors."

Avrak studied him, nodded, and put out his arm for the hand-fasting. Peganna laughed and clapped. Then she straightened on the stool and reached for the ladle in one of the cooking pots to stir it. A woman leaned forward, horrified that her queen should do her task, but Peganna waved her away.

"It has been too long since I worked for the *dravi*. Let me at least do this," she smiled. The firelight caught her features, burnishing them to a pale gold. A lock of her silver hair had fallen loose, to dangle about her shoulder.

Bran thought her the most beautiful woman in the stars. As if she sensed his admiration she turned and wrinkled her nose at him. When Avrak left to speak to some returning hunters, Bran slipped into his place.

After a moment, Peganna leaned against him.

For three weeks, Bran shared the life of the clan.

He went out with a party of hunters for rock deer. He helped a smith forge new sword-blades, working the bellows and then taking his turn at the hammer that flattened the steel which was to be a blade. He sweated and his muscles grew weary with the work he did, but he delighted in his tiredness.

He even sought out old Parkan for advice.

"Teach me what I would know," he said, and when he explained his need, Parkan took him for a tramp on the high ridges.

When Peganna questioned him as to what he did with the old man, Bran would only grin and shake his head, telling her that there were facets of Lyanirn life he wanted to know more closely. If she pouted and stamped her foot–being more queenly than she guessed and used to having her own way–he would kiss her to breathlessness and say only that it was for her own good. With this, she had to be content.

From time to time he wondered why Gron Dhu had not come here to claim his life and that of the rayanal. When he spoke of this, Peganna told him that Gron Dhu was not yet strong enough to risk an open attack on her. She was popular with the people. The soldiers served Gron Dhu but when it came to an open rupture between the clans, her brother must be more powerful than he was at present.

"Until then, we are free to do as we want, as long as we stay close to the clan tents."

Then it was the turn of Bran to question her about what she did while he went walking with old Parkan. She dimpled and laughed and would tell him only that what she did was for her own good, too. If he had his secrets, so had she.

Bran knew by the men who came and went on air-sleds that Peganna interested herself in more than the daily life of the clan. Many of the visitors wore the clan devices of the fox, the bear, the deer. They were dwellers of the lowlands and the nomads of the desert, shepherds and hunters. She sat long hours with them, always asking questions, always interested in their lives and in the happenings of those lives.

She got the answer she wanted, one night, from a youth whose skin bore the heavy tan of long sunlight. He was from the southlands where the herds grazed and sunlight was a warm blanket over lush grass the greater part of the year. The southlanders wore baggy pantaloons tucked into short leather boots, with broad belts at their middles from which hung ropes and curving swords. In their country, the shepherds went naked to the waist but in this colder clime, each man wore a fur jerkin loosely tied with leather thongs.

They had come riding up a narrow trail between the rocky slopes, five men in all, with the young spokesman at point. He was a sub-chief, Bran gathered as he came up to stand a little behind the seated Peganna, with long blonde hair tied in a tail that dangled down his back.

"–a mound with a shining thing inside it," the youth was saying. "My hound went sniffing and barking all around it. I had heard the orders of my queen that we were to investigate anything that might tell us more of the Crenn Lir people and so I dug, using my saber."

The youth looked a bit uncomfortable at that, as if it might be considered a shameful thing for a soldier-shepherd to do, but was reassured at the warm smile and understanding nod Peganna gave him. The faces of the four men at his back, sitting cross-legged as they might about one of their own campfires, did not move a muscle.

"I dug, as I say, and I found a great metal wall. I called my people, many of them, and they dug, also. We found nothing, not even a door that would let us enter if we knew the manner of its opening, but we did discover–this."

From a leather bag on the ground at his feet, the sub-chief lifted out a crystal cube. As he held it up and the fire-flames touched it so that everyone could see there was something bedded deep inside it.

He came across the little clearing and knelt to the queen, holding out the cube on a palm. Peganna took it, frowning, and stared inside it. From behind her shoulder, Bran could see the tiny figure of a man.

"A picture cube," said Peganna and would have laid the cube aside but that Bran put his hand on her shoulder so that she turned to look up at him.

"It may be more than that, highness," he said softly.

Curious, she turned it over and over in her fingers. "I see no more than a picture, Bran Magannon."

Bran was filled with an odd excitement. Long ago, on one of the worlds of Akkan, he had found such a thing, half-buried in silt near an old ruin. There had been a picture of a tree inside it which, when Bran was half asleep that night, had whispered in his mind.

He had been sleeping. The cube of the tree lay near his sleeping bag. Restless, he had turned in his sleep so that his face was touching the cube. It seemed, in that half-waking state, that words had formed in his mind from the cube. Later he had tried to cause the same effect but could not, as though the cube were worn out from much use and was simply too tired to do what it should.

He stood now with the cube Peganna handed him, smiling faintly down at it. The picture here was clear, as though formed yesterday. The picture of the tree had been a nebulous thing, faintly glimpsed as through water. The words in this cube might be fresh, strong.

His hand lifted. The cold crystal touched his forehead.

Bran cried out.

You who find this, if ever you do, know that these are the last words of Antro Zorr, chief marchical of the Crenn Lir colony of Lar. Disaster has come to my people. Nearly all are dead now. I am one of the last to be left alive, hurrying my fellow Larns to finish this mausoleum in which we bury our past.

Peganna was standing before him, eyes shining, breathing fitfully. She asked, "What was it? What happened? What did you see?"

He touched the cube to her forehead, hearing her gasp, watching her lips open wide. There was a faraway stare in her eyes as she listened to that dead voice whisper telepathically to her brain.

"A mausoleum," she breathed. "In which the Crenn Lir left mementos of their civilization. Bran, it has to be."

She whirled on the sub-chief, handing the cube to him. The youth touched it to his own head, then passed it to his fellows. It went around the campfire slowly, so that all might hear its voice.

Bran said, "It is a new cube. The one I found on the Akkan planet was old, used up. That one was probably a poem carried about by the man who lost it or threw it away when it outlived its usefulness."

Peganna made an impatient gesture. "We will go to the mausoleum, at once. Tomorrow, at dawn."

"The cube was one of many, I'd guess," Bran went on. "Left at the mausoleum to be found by anyone who came upon it. When it was built, the mausoleum might have been a splendid structure, impossible to miss."

She hit his arm with her fist in her eagerness. "Do you hear a single word I'm saying, Bran Magannon? What difference does the cube make? The mausoleum is the important thing."

His smile was humoring. "What good is the mausoleum to us when it's Gron Dhu who has the blue egg?"

She put a hand to her mouth, tears brimming up into her eyes. Her throat worked a moment, then she whispered. "Bran, are we always to know defeat? Can't we win even a little victory?"

"Why, we're alive–and the blue egg exists. All we have to do is figure a way to get it."

But she slumped in despair, so that Bran had to lead her to the little stool she used as a throne. As she sat, she sighed and lifted her face in the fire-flames He could see tears clearly on her cheeks.

"Suddenly, I'm so tired," she whispered.

His grin was hard. "Be tired, acushla. This is man's work from now on. You sit and wait." He went past her among the shepherds, talking swiftly, telling them that Peganna would be ready to travel on the morrow.

"We go by air-sled but we need directions. The queen would see the mausoleum with her own eyes. She fights for her people, does your queen–for what lies inside the mausoleum may mean the freedom of you all. A better world to live. No radiation sickness for which you need these pills."

His hand brought out a handful of the white pills so they could see them. The sub-chief growled in his throat. He hated the pills, as did all his people, but they were a way to stay alive. Bran guessed they looked on the pills as a prisoner might on the manacles that held his ankles.

As he spoke, he felt the first stirrings of homesickness inside himself. Earth lay far across the stars, forbidden to him by his own will and desire until he could come back a conqueror, a man to take his old rank of Fleet Admiral. Until now, this had only been a dream in his mind, something which had no chance at reality.

Now, however–

His fingers closed over the cube. It felt oddly warm, as though a part of the man inside it were still alive. An odd thought. And yet, perhaps not so odd. The cube might be himself, a dead thing without a world to call his own, a wanderer across the faces of the stars. Yet still alive, still warm with the unfulfilled hope that someday he could go home to Earth.

Vindicated in the eyes of the Empire.

As Commander Bran Magannon, Admiral of the Fleet.

The breath hissed between his teeth. Had the cube been less than solid it might have broken in his grip. To stand on green Earth, to sniff its scented winds and the salt air of its oceans. To walk barefoot along a seashore, to hurtle on skis along a snowy slope, to walk a city street and see the products of the stars in the store windows!

The meanest man on Earth could do all these, yet they were denied to him who had saved Earth from defeat at the hands of these people who were his hosts. Bran growled in his throat. Enough of self pity! What he must do now was find a way to make Earth take him back. Aye, and his bride who was to be, Peganna of the Silver Hair.

"The directions," he asked the youth. "How may I find the mausoleum?" As he spoke he felt Peganna touch his hand, stand beside him. Yes, she was as much a part of this quest as he was himself.

The hell with protocol! He put his arm about her shoulders and hugged her. If any of her people objected to his familiarity with Peganna, let them try and stop him. She laughed softly as if she had read his mind, and leaned her head against his shoulder.

Together, they learned the way to the mausoleum.

Dawn lay behind the jets of their air-sleds as they coursed above a series of rocky highlands. Far and far away, they could make out distant hills which once had been high mountains, blue and hazy with distance, like the goals which Bran the Wanderer and Peganna of the Silver Hair had set for themselves.

Like darting swallows they fled across the sky.

First Bran and then Peganna would take the lead in this race through space toward the tomb of a dead people. Slowly the stone ridges fell behind them and now they slipped across a rolling timber line of firs and spruces, that became a vast land of grass and dwarf pines which appeared to stretch interminably to the south. The sun was hot above them and when he could, Bran slipped out of the fur jerkin he had worn in the hills.

Something white lay on the grass in the distance, sprawling like some flattened monster out of legend. Bran grinned when he saw it was no more than a great flock of sheep grazing as wolf-dogs ran around their edges, barking at the stragglers. Now he could see the cotton tents of the shepherd clan, each striped and painted, with the history of its family.

Peganna brought her sled to the ground in a cloud of dust. Bran was not quite so accomplished with the strange carrier. He bounced three times before the wheels caught and held.

Peganna was speaking to an old man as he came up to them. The old man was nodding his head and pointing. Bran shaded his eyes.

Yes, he could see it, now. Sunlight was glinting on a piece of metal jutting up from a distant mound. The mausoleum of the Crenn Lir.

SEVEN

A PART of one metal wall had been exposed. It loomed up like an ancient rampart, silent and mysterious, its story perhaps never to be learned. Behind it was the mound that hid it, which the years and the centuries had built of loess and detritus. Tufts of grass and a few hazelnut bushes carried here by the storm winds, grew in sparse fashion across its back, dots of green against a somber brown soil.

Peganna stared at it, eyes alive as if it were a thing of beauty. Bran was more realistic. He went down into the depression carved out by the sword of the young sub-chief and kicked about among pebbles and bits of hardened dirt. It would be no mean feat to expose this bulky tomb to the rays of Miranor's sun. Many men would be needed for such a dig, and Bran wondered if the proud Lyanir would agree to bend their backs at the word of their young queen.

Still, if the people realized that they might be fighting the most desperate battle of their lives at this site, they should respond with fervor. He went to Peganna, telling her how he felt.

"Oh, they will dig," she assured him. "I told the clan of the Ax to follow me and to send riders to the clans of the fox and the wolf. Within a week this will be a tent city, Bran Magannon."

Bran studied the great metal wall, then moved back a hundred paces. "Tell your men to begin their dig here," he said slowly.

"Bran, you don't understand. I want only to expose the mausoleum. What good will it do us to begin so far away?"

"You said yourself you would put up a tent-city about the tomb, to house the men who will explore it. How large a tent-city do you imagine the Crenn Lir must have made, to house the men who built it?"

"Yes, but–"

"Death came for them, perhaps while they were still working on their vault, mavourneen. They will have left artifacts and other things from their culture behind them. Perhaps even more cubes like the one your young chief found."

"Even if we found those artifacts, it would do us no immediate good. Eventually we will, naturally, but right now the vault is the more important of the two."

Bran sighed, "What good is the vault without the egg?"

She stared at him. "Gron Dhu has the egg, Bran."

"Exactly. I mean to have him bring it to us."

Peganna sat down on the grassy slope. "Bran Magannon, you talk in riddles. If Gron Dhu comes here he will kill us both. Especially since we've gone to the trouble of finding the vault for him."

"I know that."

She laughed, almost in irritation. "Yet you want him to come with an army to fight and defeat us."

"I didn't say that. I want him to come here, it's true. As to the army and its ability to defeat us–I have other thoughts on the matter."

"What thoughts, Bran my darling?"

"None I can tell you as yet, acushla."

Her white hands balled into fists. "Bran Magannon, sometimes I could hate you! Do you realize how infuriating you are with all this mystery!"

"I want no inkling of what I have in mind to come to the ears of your precious brother. Else he might send his army and stay home himself with the egg."

She shrugged her shoulders, smiling wryly.

Bran came to her and kissed her.

On the third day of the dig, they uncovered the imprint of a human body pressed by time and the acids of slow corrosion into a length of rock. The archaeologists who had come to the summons of their queen spent long hours with delicate brushes and a plastic spray that formed a protective sheath about the fragile outline. When they were done, they announced the body to be that of an old man.

"A man, you say?" Bran asked. "A humanoid?"

"More than a humanoid. A man, as we know man to be."

They found three others, the next day, and five more the day after, and the bodies were all of old men. This made no sense, Bran protested, and the scientists agreed with him. Yet here was the proof of their words, these faint limnings of men grown old and weak, dying like flies about the tomb they had constructed.

"It was no old man we saw in the cube," Peganna murmured.

The archaeologists agreed to that, too.

The spades of the diggers turned up more than body outlines. Here they found a cluster of the crystal cubes; beyond them were metal drinking cups, apparently fashioned of an alloy that was resistant even to the ravages of time. There were pictures carved and painted on the cups, though the paint was worn so much only a few flakings were left.

A tent had been set aside for the philologists, those men who best understood the Crenn Lir language. These men and women labored over the broken shards and the cups, deciphering words, putting the crystal cubes to their foreheads to interpret the telepathic messages they carried.

The mausoleum grew into the air as the dirt around it was dug out and carted away. Its walls were rectangular in shape and still brightly gleaming, as if made from the same alloy as the drinking cups. Nowhere did they show a doorway or even a single scratch.

Three weeks after the dig had begun, the dirt was pushed away from a tiny hollow in the exact center of the mausoleum roof. Peganna was there with Bran when the hollow was revealed. She gave a little cry and fell to her knees, rubbing her fingertips into and around it.

"The blue egg will fit here, Bran!"

"Yes," he nodded. "It is time now to send for Gron Dhu."

Peganna was fearful, but she was so accustomed to follow where he led that she did no more than remonstrate with him. At his request, she sent for the young sub-chief of the shepherds.

"Orsakan, my lord would have you leave us for a little while, to pay a visit to my brother," she told him.

"That usurper," the young man spat.

"Exactly, Orsakan," Bran said. "And it is to that usurper you will desert. Hold on! No need for temper. Only hear me out. I must bring Gron Dhu here–with the blue egg. Understand this clearly.

"Understand also that if you hope to see your people on a rich planet, a world where you will not have to take pills to stay alive, your mission is of the utmost importance. Everything hinges on your ability to convince Gron Dhu that you have turned against Peganna and have deserted to his standard."

The sub-chief glanced at his queen, who nodded. Orsakan squared his broad shoulders. "If it is the wish of my queen, then it shall be my wish as well."

"You are to tell Gron Dhu that we have found what we believe to be the weapons' vault. Tell him everything you have seen here, to convince him that you speak the truth. Hold nothing back–except your loyalty to Peganna."

The young man frowned. "Gron Dhu will bring an army. He will make you and Peganna his prisoners."

"No," Bran said crisply. "He will not."

By nightfall, Orsakan was galloping a fleet darse, an animal peculiarly Lyanirn, which was a combination of a horse and a deer that put Bran oddly in mind of the mythical unicorn, across the grasslands toward distant Andelkrann. He would be a week in traveling to the ancient city. Gron Dhu would make the return trip much more swiftly, for he would bring his army by flier to the dig.

"Until then, we can go about our chores," Bran told Peganna.

Two nights later, the archaeologists sent for the queen. Bran accompanied her into the huge tent set aside for the storage of the Crenn Lir artifacts. Rising to greet their queen were the foremost archaeologists and philologists of the Lyanir.

"We know what happened to the Crenn Lir, highness," the oldest among them said. He was shaking slightly in his excitement.

Peganna took her place in a chair at the table. Bran sank down beside her, leaning elbows on the table. A few of the clan chiefs had followed her into the tent, going to the places which were theirs by long custom.

The old man, who remained standing, touched a handful of crystal cubes on the table before him. His gaze went to the shards of pottery, the drinking cups, a metal cylinder or two in which had been found metal sheets covered with the Crenn Lir writing.

"They were a great people, the Crenn Lir," the old man said softly. "In my eyes, they were the master race of all humankind. You, my queen, and you, Bran Magannon who was once my enemy, are both descended from these ancient people."

Before time began for the Earth or for the planet Lyanol, the Crenn Lir were. They had struggled up from earliest existence as a simple cellular organism in the sea, onto land and from four legs to two, with two arms. From beast they became man over unguessable ages. Once their evolving brains had become intelligent enough, they had progressed swiftly.

They were fortunate in that their solar system held other planets that were as habitable as their own. When their population exploded they went out to these worlds and from them to the planets of the nearer stars. It took a thousand centuries, but they found the way. There were individuals among them who left their names as milestones in the years. Imnalis of Vasthor, who found a way to travel faster even than the rays of light, by warping space itself. Karanthin, who bettered the discoveries of Imnalis by finding out the properties of space and time needed to perfect teleportation, and then proving his theory by building the first tele-door.

With the tele-doors, the Crenn Lir ranged their universe.

All they need do was take the materials to build a tele-door to a newly discovered planet, place it there and within seconds they had the resources of the Crenn Lir worlds at their fingertips. Their colonies ranged far through the stars.

Until–

A cruising hyper-spacer first encountered the Yann.

The spaceship vanished in a spiral of incandescent energy.

Yet the commander of that ship had sent back a report of the black vessel that had come plummeting out of the deeps of space between their universe and the next one, millions of light years away. The Crenn Lir were alerted to the fact that there were aliens in the space they ruled, invaders from another galaxy, who first destroyed without asking questions, without lifting a hand in proffered friendship.

The Crenn Lir gathered its space might and waited.

The aliens were not sighted again in our galaxy until a fleet of ten thousand ships dropped down on the planet called Ufinisthan. Their tremendous weapons wiped out the planet with all life. Then the aliens went back across the millions of light years to their own galaxy.

And the Crenn Lir began to die.

The death came at them slowly, as though the forces that gave them life were being drawn off, funneled outward into Time itself. Men who had lived at least a thousand years now lived less than fifty.

When ships were sent to desolate Ufinisthan—Deirdre? wondered Bran—they could not land because of the intense radiation that blanketed the entire world. It was this radiation that, seeping across all space, was killing off the Crenn Lir people.

When the Crenn Lir tried to land men on Ufinisthan, within hours they were dead. No man could set foot on the blasted world without dying before he could gather any information.

The Crenn Lir struck back.

Oh, yes. They marshaled their finest warships and they sent them to the galaxy of the aliens, and in a titanic battle smashed the aliens, the Yann, until not one of them was left. On the return trip, every man in every Crenn Lir ship died of old age.

"Not because of the time they took for the return voyage," said a woman philologist who had picked up the threads of the story, "but because of the radiation that had seeped into their flesh and their bones."

One thing more those warriors in the intergalactic fleet had done. They had sent back word that the only hope for life for any of the Crenn Lir lay in going to the other end of the universe, where they had never been, and there to set up colonies and hope that in time, the deadly radiation would
wear off.

This had been done. Thousands of ships had led to the more distant stars, each one carrying its cargo of men and women and children, in a vast farming of any habitable worlds they might find.

"Your Earth, Bran Magannon," smiled the woman, "and. my Lyanol are colonies of the Crenn Lir."

"There is no proof of that," Bran said slowly. "And yet my people possess ancient legends of a garden called Eden where no man was required to work, where everything fell into his hand for the asking, where there was only happiness."

"A remembrance of the Crenn Lir worlds."

"It may be so. As our notion of the snake or Satan or Devil that tempted Eve may be only an imperfect remembrance of the events that lead up to the disaster that denuded the Crenn Lir planets of life."

The woman nodded, "Yes, it could have been passed down from mother to child in the Crenn Lir ships that crossed the voids to land eventually on Earth. What generation of children first set foot on your planet or our own, we may never know."

"And if there were many so-called men living there," Bran murmured, "they must have wiped many of them out. In time, I suppose, they may have mated with the more attractive of the Cro–Magnon females. From them, in long thousands of years of time, the old Crenn Lir blood spread everywhere."

"As it did on Lyanol. We too have legends vaguely like your own. In that time, all memory of the event would have died out. Only a story would have remained."

"Of a garden called Edan," Bran smiled.

"And of a place named Aesann."

There was silence in the tent, after this. Peganna sat with her head in her hands, brooding at the crystal cubes spread out before her. Bran scowled at his clenched fists, thinking of how Empire had refused these people–their brothers and their sisters!–living room on their planets. The archaeologists and the philologists with the clan chiefs glanced about at one another, waiting for they knew not what.

Peganna laughed harshly, suddenly.

"Our forefathers died here on Miranor. We, their distant nieces and nephews, will die as well."

"Only if you choose to die," Bran told them.

When they looked at him, he added, "Can't you see it for yourselves? This is Earth history you hold here! The story of where man came from. Never has man really accepted the idea that Earth-planet was his true home. There are too many unanswered questions, too many gaps in the line of inheritance, to make it absolutely certain. I buy your explanation that the Crenn Lir are my ancestors. All Earth will buy it, too. We'll go to them–Peganna, a few of your archaeologists and philologists, and myself–with pictured proof of what these cubes and artifacts tell us. Empire will listen." His big fist rammed the tabletop, causing the cubes to dance a little. "By God, I'll make them listen!"

They were infected by his enthusiasm. Smiles and cheerful voices broke out. Men stood to walk about the little tent, conversing here and there in small groups. Bran put a hand on Peganna's forearm and squeezed it reassuringly, as if he might lend her a little of his own optimism.

She lifted her head, smiled faintly.

"You make it sound so easy. Always, you make the difficult so easy. It is a way you have."

"Actually, we are allies, Earth and the Empire and the Lyanir," he told her, and the others paused at his words to turn and stare. "The war still goes on, the war between the Crenn Lir and the aliens. Don't you understand that?"

"There are no more Crenn Lir!" a philologist protested.

"Nor are there any aliens left," Bran nodded.

His big hands made a sweeping gesture. "Out there on this planet where you live, however–those aliens are still attacking. Otherwise, you wouldn't need the pills to stay alive. Their weapons made the radiation. What difference does it make if the Crenn Lir or their sons and daughters–the Lyanir–die before those weapons? It's war, all the same."

"A one-sided war. We can't strike back."

Yes you can–at their ghosts, at their weapons."

Peganna drew a deep breath. "By that you mean it's up to the Lyanir to tell Empire the truth, to get them to realize that we are all one family, really. The family of the Crenn Lir."

"Exactly. Until that is done, the war goes on."

An old man said softly, "You have convinced me, Bran Magannon. May Kronn help you convince your own people."

Next day, there was a new air about the workers. Bran sensed it when he came to the tent opening and stood breathing in the cool air of early morning. A young shepherd ran by, carrying two spades. A woman sang as she walked off into the hills with water-jars strung over her shoulders. Three older men, talking seriously, turned and waved a greeting at the Earthman.

The clan chiefs had been busy last night. They had spread the word through the tents, told the Lyanir that they were in a war. It made no difference. It gave the young men a purpose. It even made taking the pills more bearable, since now they understood that the radiation had been caused by the alien enemies of their forefathers.

Bran chuckled. The work would go apace, this day.

And it did. By noon the last bits of ground were removed from the mausoleum so that it glittered, a massive metal rectangle one hundred yards long and forty yards wide, that seemed to be made of solid silver. This was their inheritance, Bran told them, when they were done. Inside it were the weapons and the artifacts, the blueprints and the designs, which were theirs as the sons and daughters of the Crenn Lir.

Peganna knelt down beside Bran where he stood on top of the vault, and touched the little hollow where the blue egg was to fit. "If only I held it now," she breathed. In frustration, she beat her hand against the metal lid.

As if in answer, a voice cried out.

A shepherd lifted an arm, pointed. They all could them now, like a wedge of geese against the sky, flying swiftly. Air-sleds and larger fliers, moving south from Andelkrann.

Gron Dhu had come.

Peganna called out harshly, standing proud and regal. A wind fluttered her long silver hair and rippled the hem of her short black jacket. Bran pursed his lips thoughtfully when he saw the battle light in her eyes.

"Acushla," he began, intending to say more, but her gesture silenced him,

"This is my fight, Bran Magannon. I am still rayanal of the Lyanir. Gron Dhu is the usurper."

Men ran to her call, fanning out, darting here and there into the hide tents and bringing out their weapons. Hill men and shepherds, mountain nomads and tenders of the darst herds, were ranging themselves at her back. The Lyanir were a fighting people. They recognized right when they saw it, and as Peganna had said, she was still their queen.

They waited, watching the sky.

A large flier lowered to the ground, half a mile from the metal rectangle. Gron Dhu was first off the ship, followed by his officers. Peganna waited on top of the rectangle, smiling faintly. Just so might a Crenn Lir woman have waited, bravely and with patience, for the coming of the alien death.

Gron Dhu came swiftly, kicking dust as he walked. A white kilt swung to his stride and the sword and holstered a-gun at his belt moved in rhythm to his swinging legs. He was a handsome man, a warrior, and he came as if to the the great victory of his life.

Behind him walked his soldiers, weapons at the ready.

For the space of a dozen heartbeats, Gron Dhu studied the metal vault, nodding in satisfaction. Then he looked up at Peganna on its top.

"You found it for me, Peganna. For this, you shall have life. I vow it! No man can say Gron Dhu is an unjust ruler."

"No man can say Gron Dhu is a ruler," Peganna answered.

A low growl echoed her words as the nomad clans moved forward a step. Gron Dhu stared around him; to Bran, he seemed oddly shaken at that impetuous movement.

"Are you fools?" he cried out. "I have an army at my back. You are only nomads, people of the hills and the grasslands. How long do you think you could stand before my men?"

"Long enough to kill them all," shouted a graybeard.

The soldiers behind Gron Dhu looked at one another. Many of them had relatives in the shepherd people, among the darst tenders and the hill dwellers. They had come here to arrest an Earthman, not to engage in civil war. Yet the habit of obedience was so strong in them that had Gron Dhu ordered them to mow down their own people, they might have obeyed.

Gron Dhu looked up at his sister. "Call off your dogs, sister mine. This is between Bran Magannon and myself."

"You are only a commander among the Lyanir, Gron Dhu. I am their rayanal. It is I who give the orders. Now–give submission! Throw down your weapons' belt and I shall show mercy when it comes time to judge your act of rebellion in making me your prisoner."

The young warlord barked harsh laughter. "Don't stir my anger, Peganna. I am rayanor, now. You are only a woman who used to be queen."

Bran thrust forward to stand beside Peganna. This was the opportunity he wanted. "By what authority, Gron Dhu?" he asked clearly, so all might hear his voice.

"By what–by Kronn, Earthman! You listen to me! You defeated us once out there in space with your Empire war fleet–but here on Miranor I am the power. At my word, you could die as you stand!"

"By what authority?" Bran repeated. "You are a rebel against the rightful rayanal. No more. Has Peganna signed over her rights in any document? Has the queen stepped down from her throne, giving your name as the man to ascend it in her place? No.

"You say you are rayanor Suppose Orsakan there, whom I see just beyond your elbow, were to say to this gathering, 'I am rayanor of the Lyanir!' How many of you would take him seriously?"

Gron Dhu laughed mockingly.

Bran nodded. "Exactly. It would be a joke. While Peganna lives, there is only one way. Orsakan could become rayanor against the will of Peganna."

The young warlord scowled. "There is no way! I am of the blood royal. I am a prince of the imperial house. I am not Orsakan."

"You are nothing more than Orsakan, making claims which he

111

cannot fulfill." As Gron Dhu started forward, lifting an arm to his warriors, Bran held up a hand.

"People of the Lyanir! Yes, you warriors who serve Gron Dhu, as well! Are the customs of your people illegal in your eyes?"

Ah, that caught them. Even Gron Dhu waited, staring.

Bran grinned. "The only way you can become rayanor is to engage in the ancient custom of the *dravi-kor*, the duel for the chieftainship, which, since the Queen is involved, will be a *raya-kor*."

He heard Peganna gasp beside him, knew she was turning to stare at him, though he did not look at her. He could not guess whether there was anger or laughter in her words as she said, "So! This is what you had in mind!"

She was more perceptive than her brother. Gron Dhu growled, "Peganna is a woman. I cannot fight a woman."

"You can issue the challenge–unless you're afraid."

Peganna said sweetly, "In which case I would appoint a queen's champion to meet you in open combat, brother mine."

Gron Dhu stood like a statue. As well as anyone, he knew the corner into which Bran Magannon had backed him. It had been the Earthman who had issued the challenge, no matter how it was disguised by this talk of *dravi-kors* and queen's champions. He had pointed the way for Gron Dhu, a way he must set his feet or lose the support even of his army.

The people waited, their eyes hard.

Gron Dhu looked around him. His warriors were waiting as were the nomads. The army had accepted his leadership, understanding that where a woman had failed in the fight with Empire, a man might succeed. Blindly they had followed after him, knowing his fighting qualities, even against their rayanal, believing it for the good of the people.

Yet here they found those people confronting them.

For the first time the army commanders and the warriors themselves understood that what they did was rebellion. No matter how many times Gron Dhu stated the fact, he was not the rayanor so long as Peganna lived or had not been set aside in a fitting manner.

They would have followed him to the death in a battle against a common enemy, even against their own people, if he were their rightful ruler. Bran Magannon had pointed out the truth. Gron Dhu was merely a pretender to the throne, a usurper.

"Are you afraid?" Bran called down.

The warriors stirred, waiting. Gron Dhu heard them stir and turn to one another, wondering at his silence. He was not afraid of Bran Magannon. As a matter of fact he itched to get him on the other side of a weapon, yet he was remembering the words Alvar Drexel had spoken to him, short days before Bran and Peganna had come to Miranor.

The Wanderer always finds a way. It isn't there for you or me to see– but Bran sees it.

For the first time, Gron Dhu knew doubt. The Wanderer was challenging him. The Wanderer must know a way to beat him. His flesh crawled at the thought. Until short moments ago, he had been rayanor of the Lyanir. Now he was nothing, merely a brother to the queen standing here to issue the challenge of the *raya-kor*.

"I challenge the rayanal," he said at last, slowly and heavily. "I assert my right to be rayanor I will fight to the death for that right in the *raya-kor*."

A sigh went from one throat to another. Now the eyes swung toward Peganna who put her hand on Bran Magannon. "I name Bran the

Wanderer to be my champion, to fight to the death against the challenger."

She leaned a little against the Earthman after the words were out, and he felt her shiver. "If you fail, I die, Bran! It isn't so much my own death I fear, though, as it is your own."

Bran fumbled in his belt pouch, bringing out the dice of Nagalang. He threw them high. They caught the sunlight and became mere silvery motes falling swiftly to his palm.

He held them. He opened his fingers.

The dragons of Moorn stared up at them. Peganna breathed, "The royal throw, that sweeps the board."

"Aye, woman. Nothing can top it. Remember it as I fight."

He put the dice back into his pouch and slipped out of his jerkin. Naked to the middle he would fight, as would Gron Dhu, to show the cuts, to make easy the death stroke, should it come to that.

"You'll need a sword, Bran."

"Any one will do."

"Not any one, no. Come with me."

She brought him at her heels–for some reason he was recalling the night Peganna and he had played at dice on the planet Makkador, and how this woman had won his life from him–toward her hide tent. She bent in its dimness and lifted the lid of a coffer.

"This was the sword of my father and his father before him," she said gently, unrolling a length of wool. "It was forged on Lyanol long ago."

The blade was a gray length of brightness below a cross-hilt, fully three feet in length and a little more than an inch wide, almost to its tapered point. As Bran put his hand about its braided hilt, the sword seemed to leap to his grip.

It was delicately balanced. It shimmered when he moved it, and darted like the tongue of a snake at his thrust. This was a masterpiece he held in his fingers, the highest product of a race of fighting men.

"I'll try to be worthy of such a blade," he growled, knowing humility.

"It was to have been my wedding present to you, long ago," Peganna smiled. "Take it now to defend my name."

She stepped into his arms, shivering. Bran felt her silver hair under his lips as he kissed her gently. For such a woman, with such a sword, he would fight until he died.

EIGHT

THE PEOPLE recognized the sword Bran carried in his hand to the little clearing that had been made for the duel. A sound like the whisper of a wind in tall trees moved here and there, for the people recognized his fitness to carry this blade that was named Lyrothonn, as champion of the queen. Were she a man, Peganna would use the sword. Bran carried it, in her name.

Gron Dhu grinned when he saw it.

"This too, shall be mine in a little while," he said to the Wanderer, moving forward with his blade held out.

Gron Dhu disdained to use the shield. As he waved it aside his eyes touched Bran, and the Wanderer read in them the hate and the controlled fury that said as plain as words that he wanted no shield in the way when he gave the Earthman his death blow.

Bran was satisfied. Though he had practiced the use of the shield in the clan hills with old Parkan, he was more at ease with a free left arm. He stepped forward.

As challenger, Gron Dhu would have the first blow, but–no more. They circled like strange dogs, warily, crouched over a little. Gron Dhu was a strong man with long arms and wide shoulders. There would be no easy victory over him, Bran knew–if there was to be victory at all.

The Lyanirn came in with stamping foot, his blade a slash of brilliance. Steel clanged as Bran parried and thrust in a riposte which drove the other man back on his heels. First attack had gone to Gron Dhu, as Bran had wanted. The formalities were over. It was cut and thrust now and with the clanging of the swords, reality for Bran Magannon became nothing except this man in the white-fur kilt on the other side of his sword-point Forgotten were the Lyanir onlookers, forgotten except for a corner of his heart was Peganna their queen.

The blades swung and dipped. Gron Dhu was an expert Swordsman. Had it not been for those long hours in the hills of the Ax clan, which he had spent with old Parkan, Bran knew he might have been dead three sword-strokes ago. His mind had run ahead of him when he had seen the *dravi-kor* between Avrak and the older man, and he had known then, with a surety that was a voice in his mind, this was the way to rid themselves of Gron Dhu.

Against this duel he had needed practice, and the ex-chieftain had been happy to teach him the strokes and the parries, the overhead molinellos and side-slashes that were a part of every Lyanirn duel. Slowly in the hills the way of a sword had come back to him. The old muscles, the old knowledge of thrust and riposte, had been reborn in Bran Magannon.

He pushed Gron Dhu back and back, slicing fiercely.

There was a pattern to his moves which he hoped Gron Dhu would see and understand. After every molinello he paused, affording his opponent a slight opening. Gron Dhu would take the overhead slash on his blade and Bran would seem to freeze. A quick man would disengage and drive his blade sideways at the Wanderer, then. If he were swift enough with his stroke, he ought to cut his belly open.

So far, the Lyanirn had not noticed it.

Ah, but he would, he would.

The clanging of the blades went on. Both men were wet with sweat now, though neither of them was tired. Bran Magannon owned a body of whipcord and steel, and Gron Dhu was always in condition.

Shadows grew longer as they fought, sometimes circling again so they might recover their wind. There was grudging admiration in the eyes that faced him, Bran saw, though there was no fear. This was not the easy victory Gron Dhu had pictured in his mind. He was going to have to work to be rayanor of his people. It was a fact that would make his new title all the sweeter.

The blades clashed, drew sparks. Feet sidestepped for balance, points always ready for the thrust, edges alert for the parry. No eye of all those that watched missed any stroke. This was a duel that would go down in Lyanirn history. Those who were here watching it must remember it, to tell it to those who should come after.

Gron Dhu let his eyes widen. By Kronn! The Earthman was growing tired. After his last overhead blow he had paused, seemed almost to wrench himself back into position. In that pause he should have cut sideways at his naked middle. Yes, yes. Now that he thought about it, this was a mannerism of Bran the Lucky. Always after the molinello he took breath and stood rigid in his attacking position.

Fool that he was, not to have seen it sooner!

Gron Dhu grinned. Once more he would test his discovery. He feinted, drew back, let his blade lower a little. Bran came in with the sweeping molinello. His blade rose swiftly to meet it. Sparks flew as the edges grated.

Again Bran had paused, stood helpless.

Excitement danced like fire along his veins as Gron Dhu circled his man, face to face and with his sword at the ready for the death cut. He knew now what he must do to kill Bran Magannon. Let him make just one more of those overhead slashes and he would be a dead man.

Bran came in on darting feet. His blade rose and fell.

Gron Dhu met his sword with the edge of his own. Almost in that instant, as the blades rang, the Lyanirn disengaged. Faster than the eye could follow, his sword swung straight for Bran at his navel, to slice him open, to cut him almost in half.

Steel met steel with a shocking jar that numbed Gron Dhu for an instant. Bran had dropped his hilt so that his sword pointed upward at the sky like a bar before his belly. It had been a trap! A devil trick to lure Gron Dhu into–

Bran disengaged himself from the parry and thrust forward.

His blade went into Gron Dhu deep, its reddened point standing out behind his back. They stood frozen there, dead man and living, Bran in the riposte, Gron Dhu with his blade fallen a little where it had gone when parried.

Then the Lyanirn fell face-down

Bran turned his eyes from the man he had killed to look about him, at the sky, at the great metal vault, at the people and the warriors standing and staring back at him. He wondered if they saw him as an Earthman at this moment or as the champion of their queen.

A voice rasped, "Peganna, rayanal of the Lyanir!"

It was the young chief, Orsakan. His blade was pointed skyward. A thousand more swords followed its example and a forest of steel lifted, below which Peganna came walking. Gron Dhu was dead. Long live Peganna of the Silver Hair!

The woman knelt beside her brother, made symbols with her fingers above his head which Bran did not understand. It was some sort of rite, he knew, but the weariness in his muscles was so acute it made an ache, dulling the world about him. Dazedly, he stared down at the sword Lyrothonn in his hand. The blade was redly wet with blood. Sighing, Bran knelt to cleanse it in the dirt.

Above his working fingers, Peganna looked at him.

"Thank you, Bran Magannon. You saved not only the woman who loves you but her people as well, this day." She smiled, reaching out to touch his hand with gentle fingertips. "Had Gron Dhu killed you, he would have given over the Lyanir to the Empire as payers of tribute. I can give them freedom and equality."

She put her hand in the pouch at the dead man's belt and lifted out the blue egg. Both hands she placed about it, cradling it between her fingers as though she drew an unknown power from its weight. Then her fingers parted like the petals of a flower and dying sunlight touched the jewel.

"This shall give them the freedom for which they long," she whispered. From the egg she turned her head to stare at the great vault. "Tomorrow, Bran. Tomorrow we shall go together to the vault and put the egg in that hollow and learn what it is the well of the Molween gave us."

She accepted his hand that lifted her to her feet. Holding onto the blue egg tightly, she walked ahead of him to her hide tent.

Bran slept like a tired child. And like a child he dreamed of faceless terrors in the night, of half-seen things hidden in the great vault that came out gibbering to the touch of the egg in its top. Like the mythical box of Pandora, Peganna might be freeing unknown horrors on the world about her, horrors against which there was no weapon, no way of safety.

He was covered with sweat when he woke.

Dawn lay to the east, red and faint on the horizon. The early morning air was cold as he dressed, and when he threw back a tent flap, he saw white mists along the ground. Those mists covered the bottom portions of the metal rectangle, as though they had seeped from it in a poisonous miasma.

The encampment was stirring all about him. Lyanirn warriors moved back and forth on their errands, sword chains clanking. The shepherd folk and the hill nomads moved more softly but just as purposefully. Understanding came to Bran as he watched. This was the day for which the Lyanir had waited over the centuries.

The vault held the answer to their future.

If the vault were filled with weapons, they could compel the Empire to a treaty, force it to give them planets on which to live, be accepted into its hegemony of nations and worlds as an equal. Perhaps this might be so, even if there were no weapons. Breathtaking inventions, marvels of science which neither the Lyanir nor Empire had even imagined, might do it. Man had not lost his power to bargain just because he had gone out to the stars.

Empire would be ready to make a deal, if the price were right. It all depended on what they discovered in the vault. There was a tightness in his middle, Bran found. Suddenly he had to know what secrets lay in that metal rectangle.

Perhaps death had struck the Crenn Lir down before they had the chance to put anything at all inside it. It might be an empty shell, no more. Ah, but–fate could not be so cruel! Even Subb of the Hundred Hates would have some mercy.

Just one artifact, one object to trade for living room!

A guard smiled and nodded, when Bran reached the royal tent. Peganna was sitting at a table, waiting for her breakfast. She looked radiant in a striped jersey and wrap-around black skirt, Bran thought, slipping onto the bench beside her.

"I would have wakened you," she smiled. "The blue egg is yours as well as mine. Without you I could never have found the well of Molween and so laid hands on it."

"I marvel that you can eat," he said.

She laughed. "It was to be a lesson in discipline. I asked myself, If Bran were torn with this need to open the vault, to see what is inside it, what would he do? And then I told myself, 'Why, first of all he would have breakfast, a good meal to tuck under his belt so that if he should find disappointment, at least it would not take him half starving to death.'"

A maid servant brought two platters of food to the table.

"Eat slowly," Bran said, and winced at her under-the-table assault on his shins with a sandaled toe. There was an urge in him to hurry also, but he fought it down and ate as though he had nothing ahead of him this morning but a walk in the hills.

As if to mock and taunt him with her own patience, Peganna ate even more slowly. Twice she caught him scowling impatiently at her knife and fork, and gleefully she would wrinkle up her nose and chew more slowly.

Until at last–when she ordered a third cup of steaming kalf–he lost patience and with a whoop put both hands under her armpits and swung her up over the table. She laughed delightedly. Bringing the blue egg out into her hand, she raced with him across the compound toward the vault.

The camp came out of its tents and stood watching. From the military section, three uniformed Lyanir officers strode forward. Dozens of scientists followed to the ladders and mounted with them.

As she set a foot down on the metal top of the great rectangle, Peganna caught Bran by the hand. "If it should be empty, Bran? What then?"

"It can't be empty, mavourneen," he growled.

Her hand was shaking so much that Bran had to cover it with his own as she lowered the egg toward the hollow. With thumb and forefinger she put the blue jewel in its cradle. It fitted exactly.

There was no sound, no movement.

And then–

Faintly it sounded, like the breath let out of the lungs in a long sigh. A wheeze of power, a susurrus of air. Underfoot the vault appeared to tremble and rise upward, carrying them with it. Only it was not the whole vault that had lifted in this fashion but a rounded disc twenty feet in diameter, in the exact center of which rested the blue egg. The treasure vault of the Crenn Lir lay open. Its lock had obligingly risen out of its cradle and set itself aside.

There were stairs leading into the interior.

Bran could see the treads outlined in a bluish glow that grew brighter the longer he looked down into that open circle. The Crenn Lir had placed uthium lights inside their mausoleum, lights that would activate themselves when the egg was put in its hollow.

Peganna was shaking, putting one foot forward, timidly, so that she might peer more closely into the blue brightness within the vault. She was aware of Bran's hand on her elbow, the soft syrup of his voice as he sought to still her quivers.

Then she was leaning over the edge of the opening, seeing metal spirals and twisted rods, odd loops of glittering compounds and great, towering oblongs. Her gasp was a soft cry of triumph.

"The Eldorado of the ages," breathed Bran, and gestured.

Men came running and their excitement touched off a spontaneous roar of victory from the encampment that was picked up by the warriors Gron Dhu had brought with him. Three scientists reached them first, with an officer of the rank of adkhan at their heels.

"Keep the men back," Bran told the adkhan. "Name details to lug out some of those things into the open, so all can see them. You, Pshen Wir," he told a gaunt physicist, "pick a party to go down inside the vault and have a look–and I want men who know weapons when they see them, no matter how strange they may seem."

Peganna was poised between laughter and tears as Bran went down the metal stair ahead of her, turning after one swift glance below to give her his hand. In that swift appraisal of the eyes, Bran Magannon knew they had found a treasure vault beside which gold and jewels paled to morning mists. This was Cibola and Tisingal, the vault of Angkor Wat guarded by an immense emerald Buddha, the mines of Ilmor Quan on Mars and all the fame pearls in the universe done up in one neat package.

His foot touched a metal floor and Peganna stood beside him, pressing closer, eyes wide with awe, lips a little parted to aid her hurried breathing. They stood in a forest of metal mysteries, of mechanical marvels which were the products of a million years of high culture.

"What are they? What do they do?" whispered Peganna.

"My hope is that the Crenn Lir told us, acushla. Otherwise we're no more than a poor boy looking in a window at a store full of goodies, with no way to get inside."

A scientist on the metal stair cried out softly. "Oh, by Kronn! I must be dreaming. Is it real?"

Bran moved toward a metal cone that rose twenty feet into the air, slapping its side. "It's real. They're all real. Only God knows what it is they do, though."

They saw only shapes and sizes, some large and some small, with a bewildering array of discs and rods and filaments interwoven back and forth to make a fairy forest. There were tiny artifacts that fit into the hand and there were others that would need a crane to budge.

The uthium bulbs made everything as clear as daylight so that as far as vision went, they could see whatever they wanted. It was what was inside the structures that puzzled them. Bran lifted a rod that held a series of thin diamond panes inset with microelectronic plates and wires. He touched the diamond panes, set them to spinning.

A blackness, grew about the Wanderer, spreading outward.

He could see inside that darkness as though he peered into violet haze, but they could not see him. Peganna looked startled, frightened, as the black blotch grew. Then Bran stilled the spinning panes and everything was as it had been.

Peganna asked, "What is it?"

"My guess is that it shifts the dimensional planes a little, refracting reality. I could see you. You couldn't see me. On a dark night, an assassin equipped with one of these things could have a ball."

"And this, Bran Magannon? What do you make of this?"

He walked with Peganna toward the scientist who had spoken, who stood beside a red spiral that climbed almost to the metal ceiling, set in a base of black stone that glittered as if it held the stars. There were levers in the black stone, and unknown symbols, with studs set for pushing. Staring at the thing, lacking understanding of its function, Bran shivered. There was something–deadly–about that crimson spiral.

"Don't touch it," he breathed. "It might be able to turn us all into no more than drifting dust motes, and the whole planet as well for all I know."

He glanced about him as if seeking inspiration. There were transparent prisms and dull gray obloids, metal eggs and towering cylinders. This might be a playhouse for mad children, or for men more sane than any who now walked the star-ways His eyes came back to the eggs.

The blue egg was a key, of course.

Might not these other eggs be keys, as well?

Some were large, too heavy to carry alone, for he tried it until his muscles bulged. But he went to a row of smaller eggs, lifting a pale green one into his palm. It was a jewel, similar to the blue egg that lay in its lock-hollow above him. Bran studied the egg, then turned and looked about the room.

Ah, just beyond that truncated cone, a pale green hexagon with a tetrahedron of bright rose above it in which black lights twinkled. Bran took the egg to the hexagon and fumbled on its surface. Yes, here.

He touched the egg to the hollow and released it.

The voice was gentle, sad, as it entered his mind.

You have found the treasure house of the Crenn Lir. To you, then, do we leave the products of our greatest minds, over ten thousand centuries of scientific progress. This instrument you see before you is a protonic transversal capable of shifting any object, living or dead, animate or inanimate, out of our universe into a dimension of null-matter.

Upon its appearance in the null-matter universe, the object ceases to exist. It is not destroyed. It just ceases to be. Where no-matter is a norm, matter itself is impossible.

To operate the . . .

The voice went on speaking slowly, softly.

A hand-touch as his shoulder made Bran turn toward Peganna. Smiling, the Wanderer lifted out the egg, then told Peganna to replace it. Now the Voice spoke to her, perhaps because of sympathetic vibrations set up within her brain by the handling of the egg.

When the voice was done, Peganna stood enraptured.

"We are babies next to the Crenn Lir," she breathed.

"Why not? Aren't we their children?"

Her smile was brief, as though her mind were on other things. "I would hate to turn such a weapon against the Empire, Bran Magannon. I hope I never have to. Yet I would. I will–unless they see reason!"

He did not say to her that this one weapon was enough of a weight to tip the scales of controversy in her direction. If for no other reason than that the protonic transversal made the most ultimate of garbage disposal units. Dangerously radioactive elements could be eliminated instantly. Slums–there were slums even on mother Earth, and conditions grew worse the farther out into the stars a man went–could be nullified and the ground built on to make housing units. The atmospheres of certain poison-planets might be drained of the noxious elements in their air, opening a thousand new worlds to colonization.

Why, with this–Peganna could pick and choose her own homeland.

But maybe it wasn't that simple.

Otherwise the Crenn Lir would have cleared their own worlds of the deadly radiation. Perhaps with more study, a way could be found to do this, to whisk away deadly radiation. The Crenn Lir might not have had time for such a study.

"And this, Bran Magannon," said another voice.

An older man stood beside a thin lemniscate of white wires, a delicate figure-eight balanced on its side above a magnetic field that held it motionless. Bran took the white egg from the grimly smiling scientist and touched it to the hollow.

. . . *dionesthenic gyrosentializer which opens up the warp-ways of the universe so that a man may stand here on Thrann and look away as far as Mawznor. To operate, touch the red stud . . .*

The voice went on, not in the words which Bran knew but in thoughts and images which he might recognize. The Crenn Lir had been farsighted enough not to leave an oral record but a mental one, probably composed by one of their most expert telepathists.

He leaned down and touched the stud.

Instantly the lemniscate began to revolve, slowly at first, then more swiftly, until it was a blur that deepened in color from white to crimson, to blue and then to white again that was shot with lavender streakings. Slowly the streaks coalesced, grew wider, larger. The oval was a lavender haze now, and then it was gone. In its place was a segment of black space, space so dark that it seemed almost alive.

The space between the galaxies, finder of the vault. Beyond the blackness and far, far away, are what were once the homelands of the Yann.

Watch!

The blackness remained unchanged for a few seconds. Then there was a wink of light, a brightness. And another. Another. It was as though Bran Magannon stood in a spaceship that went faster than a thousand times the speed of light. He was approaching a galaxy.

Dimly he knew Peganna was beside him and the others, all frozen into the moment of staring upward where the whirling lemniscate showed them this distant realm of stars that held the enemies of the Crenn Lir. There were many stars now, uncounted millions of them, making a blue-white spangle across the darkness of space. The stars grew into giant suns and went away.

Somehow, the controls of the gyrosentializer were set to show whoever opened the vault the Yann worlds. Perhaps the creators of the vault feared that their war fleet may have missed a planet, that some of the Yann might still be alive. This was to guard against surprise attack. But there were no more Crenn Lir left. Only their children, standing here in awe and wonder.

A star neared, slowed its headlong pace. Then the star was gone and now a planet showed, round and blue, its atmosphere a haze about it. The lemniscate dipped down to skim above its surface.

Black rocks and red dust desert. No more.

Everywhere the eye looked, there were only rocks and dust, with not even a slim needle of metal to show where once the high spires of the Yann had lifted proudly to the skies.

This is the homeland of the Yann, who came and attacked the Crenn Lir, for no purpose and without provocation. Life has ended here. Or— has it? Only you can know, finder of the vault. If all you see is black rock and red sand, then the triumph of the Crenn Lir is complete. I hope, for your sake, it is so.

Bran told the others what the voice in his brain had said. He wondered if his voice were as sad as the thoughts he listened to.

From one planet, the lemniscate went to another and a third. A fourth, a fifth, to a dozen different worlds. All of them were the same. There was no life. The Yann had been obliterated.

Bran sighed and put an arm about Peganna.

Above their heads the lemniscate was turning blue and crimson, then the pallid white of inertia. Its rotation slowed, ended.

The scientist lifted the white egg and held it.

"They were gods," he said gently.

"Kronn," exclaimed Bran suddenly. "The Kronn you worship! Might it be a corruption of the 'Crenn' in Crenn Lir?"

The scientist shrugged and put the egg in its proper place on a rack. "We will never know, Earthman."

Suddenly Bran froze, holding Peganna, and felt her stiffen.

Beyond the vault, the alarm was sounding.

NINE

THE LYANI-HORNS were braying like monsters in agony.

Bran caught Peganna by a wrist, whirling and bringing her with him to the metal stair and out of the vault to warm sunlight and the sweet, clean smell of air. Here and there on the high places of the encampment, men were standing with the spiraled horns to their lips, sending out their call.

It was a scientific irony that lyani-horns should sound above the vault that held the wizardries of the Crenn Lir. The horns were a way of life of a dawn civilization; the vault was an end product of countless millennia of high culture.

And yet–

It was not the fault of the Lyanirn that they must blow horns to alert their people to danger, Bran knew. The Lyanirn were long centuries of space travel away from their home world. They were the descendants of the scientists who had made the spaceships for that journey and given them the weapons with which they had fought off the Empire before Bran Magannon had been sent to take command against them. Was it guilt in the Wanderer that sent a stab of pity through him as he listened to those brayings? He did not know.

Peganna asked, "What is it?"

An officer came at the run. "A space feet, highness. Marked with the star cluster of the Empire." His dark eyes swung on the Wanderer accusingly.

Bran said, "Fight it off in a delaying action until we can get a couple of those weapons out of the vault."

The officer shook his head. "The fleet was passed through by Gron Dhu's men at Andelkrann. It is over the planet, now."

The man flushed as Bran and Peganna looked at him. He spread his hands in a plea for understanding. "Gron Dhu made a pact with the Empire commander, with Alvar Drexel. He promised us a better world as a result. We listened to him and followed where he led."

Peganna gestured impatiently. "It makes no difference–now. The damage is done. The Empire probably sent a war fleet here to bring us back to Earth, Bran. As a compliment to your former high rank, perhaps. Or to my own importance." Her laughter was bitter. "Had it come a week from now, we would be ready for it."

Bran snapped orders to the officers. There was still a chance, a bare hope, if they could get a couple of the weapons out of the vault. The tetrahedron with the black lights in it, for instance. It could hurl an entire war feet into the null universe, he was sure.

They needed time to study it, to discover its operation.

Alvar Drexel would not give them time. He would bring his space fleet here above the encampment, and out of range of the hand-weapons the Lyanir carried he would make his demands. If they were not obeyed he would destroy all.

Bran scanned the blue sky and saw only clouds and a few birds wheeling, dipping in their gliding flight. Time became an equation in which safety came up equal to an empty sky.

"Get busy," he growled, and ran to help.

In the vault, Bran and twenty more men hand-wrestled the heavy pale green hexagon with the rose tetrahedron above it, moving it slowly and with much grunting toward the opening. The Crenn Lir had a better way to do this, he was sure. There were tools, some sort of lifting beam, a gravity nullifier, perhaps, somewhere here in the vault; but he could not spare the precious minutes to go looking for it.

They had to pause to push other objects out of the way. Any of these cones and rectangles, oblates and rhomboids might serve the purpose instead of the protonic transversal; again, he could not go seeking among them. He had to make do with what he understood, at least in part.

He put the egg in the hollow so that the recorded thoughts of the Crenn Lir telepath could come to him. He learned that to operate the black lights inside the rose tetrahedron, he must open a panel in the hexagon, turn the dials and the controls set there for manual working. Ah, and aiming the tetrahedron was a matter only of turning it so that its widest facet faced the object to be nulled.

The circle of blue sky they could glimpse through the opening in the vault ceiling came nearer. Sweat ran down their backs and the breath in their lungs turned to fire. Now ropes were being lowered on pulleys over the rim to be fitted about the weapon.

Bran lifted his head once to take a deep breath, seeing those dangling ropes and straps as fingers waving him on. Hurry, hurry! they called. Alvar Drexel is on his way and you know that he is an impatient man. He will be driving his men and the engines of his spaceships to full capacity.

He will know where to come, too. The men in Andelkrann, still believing Gron Dhu to be alive and rayanor of the Lyanir, would have had no reason not to tell him. Yet for that very reason perhaps, Alvar Drexel would not know the need for haste. He would come to his ally Gron Dhu, believing him to be still in command of the Lyanir.

The pale green hexagon slid into position. Bran lifted the egg from its hollow and put it in his belt pouch. Then he caught one of the hanging ropes and began to wind it about the weapon.

"Haul away," he said at last.

The ropes tautened. A winch creaked complainingly, somewhere up above. Slowly–Kronn, how slowly!–the weapon lifted. An inch, two inches of the ground it went, swaying in its net of hempen strands. Bran put a palm to it, as if to speed its upward progress.

The thing was heavy, maybe too heavy for the crude crane to lift out into the air. The ropes hummed.

"Take it up! Take it up!" he bellowed.

"Too late, Bran," cried a voice.

A face peered over the rim at him: Peganna of the Silver hair, with disaster written on her features. Bran felt his heart give a big lurch.

"The fleet?"

"On the horizon. Lookouts sighted it far off and relayed the news by the lyani-horns. The war feet is only at a cruising speed, otherwise it would have been here long ago. I guess Alvar Drexel expects to see my brother waiting for him."

Bran rasped a curse and caught one of the taut ropes, going up its length hand over hand to the circled opening. He caught the metal rim and yanked himself up to stand beside the rayanal.

Her finger pointed northward.

He could see them now, tiny black dots that grew steadily, the closer they came. Soon they were large enough to show their outlines and Bran recognized five huge battle-wagons, half a dozen cruisers, a dozen smaller scouters. Any one of them could wreck the encampment here with a score of well-placed blasts.

There was a pain in his middle, behind his belt buckle. To have come so far, and now to fail! The injustice of the thing was a bitterness on his tongue. He wondered in an insane moment if he could use the rose tetrahedron, even now. Of course he might destroy the vault ceiling, hurling it into the null world, yet also he would obliterate the Empire war feet as well, with the same beam.

It could be worth trying!

He was turning toward the metal staircase when Peganna caught his arm. She had seen the stark fury in his eyes and asked, "What would you do?"

When he told her, she shook her head. "We dare not risk it, Bran. A beam from that–that thing below us might wipe out half my people. You would have to tilt it, prop it up for the correct angle of fire. It might topple over–even blow to nullity the rest of the vault."

She shuddered at that thought and her fingernails were claws set in his wrist. She shook him gently, "It is better if I bargain."

"You can never bargain with Alvar Drexel. I know the man."

She would not release him and he would not use force against her. Frozen in that little tableau they watched the Empire feet loom enormous in the sky above their heads. Black shadows from those titanic bulks lay like night over the vault and the encampment.

Bran had never appreciated how big the Empire spacers really were, until this moment. Their dark shadows matched his black despair.

From the flagship came a two-man flier, slim and streamlined, with a tiny compartment for its pilot and his companion. A narrow rod welded to its underpart widened into a thick lens which was the firing end of an atomic ray. The lens was aimed right at the man and woman on the vault as the flier gently lowered.

A Fleet captain stepped from the flier. He was a young man, one of the eager cadets newly risen in the Service. Bran did not know him. His white uniform was spotless, its gold braid and campaign medals, leather a-gun holster and military boots glittered with polish. Peganna he saluted, Bran Magannon he ignored except for one quick, side-wise glance.

"I am here to announce your formal arrest, by orders of Commander Drexel of the flagship *Taliesin* of the Empire space feet assigned to sector 834. You will hold yourself in readiness to be taken aboard the ship within the hour."

"Not quite as fast as all that," Bran said softly.

The officer drew himself erect, chin in and shoulders rigid. "I am instructed to tell ex-Commander Magannon that he also is under arrest, according to the Articles of Space War, section 143."

"Are you now?" asked Bran with a grin. "Son, you go back and re-read that section and while you're at it, read over 149 as well."

The eyes darted at Bran, widening slightly. "One forty-nine, sir?"

"Yes, that would be the right passage, I believe. It has to do with officers who have risen to the rank of admiral, past or present. You go back and read it over, then come see me."

Almost instinctively, the officer saluted and turned on a heel. He went back to the flier, nodded to his pilot, and was taken up in a rising spiral to the *Taliesin*.

Captain Bettencourt shivered as he climbed out of the flier onto the deck of the flagship. In an aside, he told his pilot, "The old man'll have my hide. He hates Magannon worse than poison."

A lift took him to the bridge, where he stood at attention, relating what had taken place. Drexel scowled blackly when his recitation was at an end.

"One forty-nine? What the hell is section one forty—"

An orderly ran for the service manual, flipping pages. His eyes scanned the close print, and his lips twitched. He said softly, "It says here that—"

"Don't interpret it for me, man. Read the damn thing."

"I quote, sir: Any officer of the rank of admiral, past or present, brought before any tribunal, must be accorded all the privileges of his office, except that of direct command.' I unquote, sir."

"Oh my God," breathed Alvar Drexel.

He stared at Captain Bettencourt and the orderly. He had intended to bring Bran Magannon back in chains in the hold of the *Taliesin*. Instead, he would not only have to grant him the courtesy of a stateroom but detail an orderly to attend him, see that he had uniforms and campaign ribbons, even a dress sword if he wanted it.

"The purpose of the section is to show that the post of feet commander is so important that even if arrested–"

"I know the whys and wherefors, captain! It's just that I–I'd forgotten about one forty-nine. Damn his eyes! Magannon didn't forget. Go down and tell him he shall be accorded all the courtesies. And–ask him what that metal box is he's standing on."

"Yes, sir. At once, sir."

When Captain Bettencourt stood again before Bran Magannon and the queen of the Lyanir he was more respectful. He stood at attention just as he had done before Alvar Drexel.

"Commander's compliments, sir. You shall be extended all the courtesies. Commander requests that you and the queen of the Lyanir come aboard, sir."

"Under truce?"

"Yes, sir. Under truce."

Captain Bettencourt resisted the inclination to grin. This Bran Magannon was everything rumor and legend said he was. Old timers had told the captain how Admiral Magannon had always been able to think his way out of any difficulty. He would be a match for the Old Man, all right. He never missed a trick. This might be fun, in a way.

A scouter was sinking toward the vault.

Bettencourt asked, "What is this thing, sir? Begging your pardon, sir, but Commander Drexel asked me to find out."

"I'll tell him myself, captain," Bran smiled.

Bran escorted Peganna across the roof of the vault to a metal ramp being lowered by the scouter. Under his breath he told her to leave the talking to him, other than the obvious things. He warned her not to be surprised by what he did or said.

"I am always surprised by what you do, Bran. But I promise not to show it."

Three uniformed Marines waited in the ten-man scouter. They saluted crisply and one of them escorted them to twin lounges. They were barely seated when the *Taliesin* towered overhead and the ramp was sliding out again.

Commander Drexel was in his quarters, seated behind a large desk when his visitors entered. His grin was wolfish as he rose to his feet and bowed.

"You shall be accorded every courtesy as my prisoner. I–"

"Go back, go back, Alvar," said the Wanderer with a grin. "We are no prisoners of yours."

Drexel laughed. "Are you not? Suppose I turn my rayers on the Lyanir below?"

"Even you aren't that much of a fool."

"Gron Dhu would support me. He and I have an agreement."

"My brother is dead," said Peganna softly.

The Commander goggled at her. Slowly he sank back into his desk chair, aware that his forehead was beading with sweat. If he had no ally among the Lyanir, what he had done amounted to an act of war. He had brought a battle fleet into a planetary atmosphere and by those same Articles of Space War which Bran Magannon quoted so glibly, this was a breach of the peace.

It was as if Bran followed his thoughts. "You overreached yourself, Alvar–as you always do. The best and safest course to follow now would be to submit an official apology, fill your water tanks as an excuse against your violation, and take off."

Commander Drexel sneered, "Your very excellent advice might apply were this a planet of the Empire Federation, Magannon. This is an alien world. It has not been claimed by the star cluster."

"All the more reason for caution, then. Check your manual, Alvar."

Commander Drexel felt he had been buffeted about long enough. His palm slapped the tabletop. "I know the manual! This case has no place in it. The Lyanir were enemies. May still be our enemies. It calls for a new ruling." His teeth worried his upper lip as he concentrated.

Peganna chafed under the restraint Bran had placed on her. Love him as she did, she was still queen of her people. Miranor was her world, the planet which she ruled. She leaned forward in the chair to which she had been ushered upon entering the cabin.

"Bran Magannon and I intend to come to Earth anyhow, Commander."

"Ah, do you now? And why?"

Bran said warningly, "Peganna!"

She ignored him. The mockery in the face of Alvar Drexel was as a goad to her pride, causing her to lift her head in the regal manner with which she faced her own people.

"Because I have something now to trade for living space. A vault of scientific marvels. A metal rectangle filled with the–"

"Peganna!"

"Filled with what, your highness?"

The silky voice of the Fleet Commander should have warned her but she was beyond caution. She was a ruler of a proud people. It was not in her heritage to bow and scrape before any man. She erupted out of the chair and stood with arms by her side, her eyes blazing.

"Filled with marvels neither you nor I have ever seen! Even my own scientists find themselves like children in the vault. The knowledge of the Crenn Lir is to ours as ours is to a cave civilization. It is my intention to offer these marvels to the Empire, share and share alike, as equals."

"No doubt, no doubt," muttered Drexel.

Bran moved like a panther, coming beside Peganna and catching her arm, squeezing it with his strong fingers until she winced. His smile was cold as he turned it on the man who had been his subordinate in the years when he had worn the star cluster on his uniform.

"As long as the pot's been kicked over, I'll tell you more, Alvar. You have the chance to be a hero–or a fool. Take us with honor to Earth and you'll get any reward you want. The vault is that breathtaking."

Commander Drexel came close to goggling. He knew Bran Magannon as well as any man might know him. He was no weather-vane to shift about with every breeze. If Bran Magannon thought the vault was that wonderful, why then–"

His eyes narrowed. His finger pressed a stud of the control panel inset into his desktop. "There will be weapons in the vault, I assume." His eyes were on Peganna as he spoke, and when her eyelids flickered, he knew he had struck home.

"Yes, weapons. Weapons on an alien world–an unfriendly world inhabited by the one-time enemies of Empire. It makes a difference. Oh, yes, quite a difference."

A door opened. An ensign stood waiting, back rigid.

"Put these two in irons, Broome. Then have a scouter waiting alongside the deck for me. I'll go down and examine the vault myself."

Drexel seemed to bloat with triumph as he stared at Bran Magannon. "I have ways to make men talk, Bran Magannon. I won't bother to use them on you or the wench with you. There'll be Lyanir scientists below who won't hold out their information on me."

He turned his back on them and moved toward the doorway. Peganna moaned softly and turned an imploring face up at the Earthman. "Bran, Bran! You told me to say nothing. I–I couldn't help myself."

"It's done, mavourneen."

"What can he do if he finds a way to get into the vault and–and learns what some of those things can do?"

"As he said. He'll take us to Earth as prisoners."

Her haunted eyes searched his tanned face. "Then there isn't any hope at all?"

"None I can see, acushla."

She might have crumpled except that his arm was about her middle, holding her upright. Bran stared down into her pallid features and whispered hard oaths under his breath.

An ensign took them in the middle of an armed escort down into the hold of the huge spacer and locked them in a room with metal walls, with two cots at either end, with a table and two chairs riveted to the floor. The air was clean and scented. Normally, this was the quarters of a spaceman first class. For a while, it would be their home.

Peganna threw herself on the nearer bunk and, folding her arms over her face, began to weep very softly. Bran stared at her, wanting to comfort her yet finding no words with which to do it. Drexel was right. Weapons in the vault–and Kronn knew there were weapons!– would make a difference.

Commander Drexel would be a hero, all right. His claim would be that he had ferreted out a weapons vault on the Lyanirn planet of Miranor, that he had made a swift descent before those weapons could be trained on his feet–and captured them. Otherwise, he would say, with those vault weapons the Lyanir could have smashed the Empire without stirring off its planet.

He was right. This was the frightening part of it. In the eyes of the Empire and its uncounted billions of people, he was absolutely correct. When word of what those marvels could do was spread across the Empire, a breath of relief would go up that would shake the star cluster standards from Acamar to Zosma.

He sat down hard on the closest chair.

Right now Drexel would be on the vault roof, asking questions. There would be torture if no one told him about the blue egg. Ah, and then–he would learn all he wanted to know about the vault.

Bran shivered. Though he had never employed torture himself as a Commander, he had served as captain under a brutal officer who was given to the use of a nerve stimulator–official equipment for the neuro-surgeon on board ship–on a spy or two he had got into his hands. The nerve stimulator at its highest pitch could say sensitive nerve ends like a tiny whip. No man could stand up to that pain, which made no mark except in the lines of a man's face when he screamed.

The Lyanirn would talk, Kronn help them."

And their every word meant death for Peganna and himself.

He put his head in his hands.

He sat there a long time. Two hours or three or even four, it made no difference. The dead cannot stir and walk about. He roused to the opening of his quarters door. Four Marines with drawn a-guns came in and lined up with their backs to the wall. At least he does me the courtesy of being afraid, Bran reflected. Then Commander Drexel entered to stand before him.

Drexel tried to speak and could not, at first. Only his brilliant eyes and the high flush in his cheeks told of his excitement, of the faming success he had achieved. Slowly he reached into the pocket of his white uniform jacket and lifted out the blue egg. He tossed it up and caught it.

"Traitor," he said then, to Bran Magannon.

On a heel he swung toward the bunk where Peganna lay with an arm flung across her eyes. "Enemy ruler," he whispered softly.

Then he snarled, "By all the gods of space! I knew some day I'd get you where I wanted you, Magannon! Ah, you can't guess how it feels, to stand here and see you a broken man.

His fist slapped into his cupped palm, again and again. "As a traitor, you'll stand trial. You haven't a chance. You know what they do to traitors? They hang them high.

"As for your queen, your precious Peganna–she'll be executed, too. Oh, not the rope. Too undignified for a woman. They'll gas your floozy."

Bran went over the table, vaulting it with widespread legs and with his palms flat on its top, as if he were playing leapfrog. His action was so sudden, the four Marines could only gape. Then his head was ramming into Alvar Drexel's face and as they went down in a heap the uniformed men dared not fire for fear of hitting their commander.

Bran lifted a hammer-like fist and rammed it into the face beneath him. He hit it three times, great swinging blows with every ounce of his strength behind them, before the Marines caught his arms and dragged him free.

Instantly Bran subsided. He had nothing against the servicemen. "Take him the hell out of here," he told to the four. "And remind him that even prisoners of war are safe from insult."

They carried an unconscious Alvar Drexel from the little cabin and the door clanged shut behind them. From her bunk, Peganna stared at Bran where he rubbed his knuckles.

"That was foolish, darling."

"But very satisfying."

"He'll hate you more than ever."

"He's done his worst, already. He won't fog me or anything like that. This isn't a barbarian Empire, for all its faults. He has to feed me and keep me healthy–to stand trial. He wants me to kick air, does Commander Drexel, though if it were up to him, he'd find another punishment."

There was a little silence.

Then Peganna asked wistfully, "Do you hate me so very much, Bran? If it weren't for my mouth, we wouldn't be in this trouble."

He laughed and came to sit beside her, touching her silver hair with a gentle hand. "Acushla, you are a queen. As a queen you answered him. I was proud of you–even while I cursed the tongue that put us in his power."

She snuggled closer to him, saying, "A lesser man would rant at me, Bran Magannon."

His only answer was to kiss her.

In his quarters, Commander Alvar Drexel lay in sleep while a surgeon patched his broken face. A neurasthetic had killed the pain that greeted his first waking moments. His nose was broken and his cheekbone had been splintered, so that he would lie here for most of the voyage, helpless. A captain would assume command in his absence.

From time to time, long after the bandages had been wrapped about his head, he would rouse from the induced slumber in which he lay, and stare upward through the bandage slits at his ceiling. He could see only a small section of the ceiling, but it was enough. It was his anchor to reality, to the fact that the *Taliesin* and the war fleet were hurtling through hyperspace toward Earth and his own ultimate victory.

Under the bandages his lips would smile.

He had a stranglehold on his old enemy. Photographs of the mysterious objects in the weapons vault–now locked against the coming of Empire scientists, with the blue egg placed securely in the ship's safe–were to be exhibit one in the case against Bran Magannon.

This was one time the Wanderer would not wriggle free. There was no way out of the trap.

TEN

WORD HAD gone on ahead of the *Taliesin*.

By ultranibeam, the communications center of the flagship had alerted the High Council of the Empire that it was bringing back ex-Admiral Bran Magannon and the queen of the Lyanir to stand trial. They had uncovered the lost secrets of an unknown master race in the stars, and with it had intended to make war on the Empire. The swift action of Fleet Commander Alvar Drexel had nullified all their plans.

In substance, this was the message which Alvar Drexel had dictated from his sick bed. It was flashed from the *Taliesin* to the receiving sets of a thousand Empire worlds. All space knew almost at the same moment that Commander Drexel had saved the people of those worlds from a holocaust of destruction.

The gratitude of these billions was only to be guessed at, Drexel knew. He would be feasted and honored from now on, everywhere in space.

The warmth of that knowledge helped to heal him.

When the *Taliesin* approached Luna, a fleet came out to meet him, flashing its colors in tribute, ranging alongside the flagship and acting as escort to the unloading platforms on the moon. A hundred newsmen from the star papers, a score of television cameras, were on hand to record the landing of the arch-traitor and the woman for whom he had renounced allegiance to the star cluster.

As they walked side by side across the domed platform, a target for eyes and lenses, Bran Magannon told himself that they cut a sorry picture. His garb was the ocana-fur kilt and broad leather belt which had been the companions of his wanderings. Peganna, though she walked like the queen she was, was in despair at her grimed skirt and jersey.

145

"We look like half-drowned pups," he told her.

She nodded through the tears of impotent shame and anger in her eyes, following the escort detail into a launch-site where a small spacer waited to carry them to Earth. Glancing up, she could see the blue-green bulk of Earth and pick out its oceans and its continents. This was the world which had defeated her, this the planet which had sent its sons and daughters into space to form colonies and then the Empire. It was her bitterest enemy.

There would be no mercy on the Earth for Peganna of the Silver Hair, nor for the man who walked beside her. Guiltily, remembering it had been her tongue that had brought them here, she glanced at Bran Magannon.

His face was hard, as though chiseled out of mahogany. Forgotten was the fact that this man had once saved the Empire himself. Remembered only was his present guilt.

They entered the metallic launch building. Their footsteps rang with hollow insistence on the ramps and stairways taking them up to the sleek spacer. Men in the white uniforms of the Empire Fleet were everywhere. There was no emotion on their faces, other than a kind of awe when they looked at the Wanderer. He was a legend in his own lifetime, and now that more and more of his story was being told, the magnitude of what he had done was being assessed and slowly understood.

A spaceman took them into a lounge and left them. The spacer had been insulated with contra-gravitic strips so that it could come and go from Earth with no more unpleasantness than that of a motorboat pulling away from a quay.

Peganna walked to the viewing screen and watched as the motors rumbled to life. The great domes of Luna, of transparent plasticene, enclosed the great compound of moon-surface which had been covered over in the centuries since man had first made a landing here by acres upon acres of buildings and cultivated gardens.

She would not have liked to live here all her life, but she understood from what Bran had told her that Moon-base personnel was shifted every three months. It made a return to Earth all the more pleasant after such a time of breathing manufactured air and walking within a restricted enclosure.

Earth grew larger in the screen. It became mammoth against the backdrop of black space and pale stars, until it filled the screen and the haze of atmosphere replaced sharp outlines. In the far distance the horizon made a curve where Florida jutted across the sea toward the island of Cuba. Then they were sweeping lower, across the green bulk of Central America and Mexico, the retro-gravitic plates warming to their task of slowing the swift glide.

Fliers lifted to meet the spacer, to escort it toward a vane-down at the astroport. As the ground grew into buildings and slim, high towers, Peganna turned from the screen to bury her face against Bran's chest.

"Until now it has been only a nightmare to me," she whispered. "This is the waking-up part, the reality."

"It will seem endless for a few weeks," he said. "Then it will be over."

She smiled up at him through her tears.

Her face was the dream that had filled his own mind in the past years, since he had known her. These quivering lips he had kissed, this long silver hair, disarranged now so it hung down her back, these brave eyes behind their tears, were all he asked of life. Now even this was to be denied him.

A black rage filled Bran Magannon.

Almost instantly it disappeared, replaced by as terrible a despair. The only hope for the Lyanir, for this woman and himself, lay in the metal treasure vault of the Crenn Lir. And that was in the hands of the Empire. A fleet would be dispatched there—was even now on its way through hyperspace with the blue egg, no doubt—to rifle its contents, to load them on huge space traders and bring them back across the gulfs of emptiness to Earth.

Nothing was left to them. Nothing!

The Lyanir might fight but they could not hold out long against the Empire, especially if Empire got its hands on the weapons in the Crenn Lir vault. Without Peganna, without her brother to take command in her place, they were a beaten people.

And Peganna, leaning against him, was a beaten woman.

He could sense the defeat in her bonelessness, in the apathy with which she reacted to his squeeze. He told her, "There is always hope." As if to deny it, she shook her head and turned away toward the opening door.

The spacer was setting down on Earth soil now, its gravitic plates humming softly, sending a throb through the ship. Peganna straightened her shoulders. She would go to her doom as befitted a queen of the Lyanir.

Chin high, she moved ahead of Bran Magannon.

There were a thousand reporters at the astroport, lined up and relaying back their stories by special wave-length, with microphones strapped to their chests. Televiewing cameras dollied in on the man and woman emerging from the spacer hatch. Hand cameras clicked steadily, like the pulse-beat of metallic hearts.

The thousands of men and women behind the silvered chains were silent, just staring. There were no hisses or catcalls, nor boos and jeers. It was as though the crowd realized the danger it had been in from the Lyanir and, now that the threat was over before it had really begun, wanted to see those who had caused it.

There was only one incident. They were almost at the waiting air-car that would whisk them above the traffic lanes on official business, when a woman cried out to Bran Magannon.

"Forget her, Admiral. We haven't forgotten how you saved us from her kind, years ago. She is a witch! Renounce her!"

The cry was echoed all across the field.

"Renounce her! Renounce the witch!"

Ahead of him, Peganna squared her shoulders. Bran chuckled, moved up beside her, and put his arm around her. The crowd fell silent at his action. And so, like that, they came at last to the air-car and stooped to enter it. A guard in another compartment with an a-gun trained on them was to ride as escort.

The air-car slid from the astroport twenty miles above a crowded highway, where magnetic grids kept the automatically controlled ground-cars at a steady sixty miles an hour. Through the transparent roofs of the cars below, they could see people looking up at them, noticing the star cluster engraved on the underbelly of the air-car, knowing them for the traitor and the Lyanir temptress come to Earth for judgment.

As if those upturned eyes were an intolerable weight, Peganna whimpered in protest. Bran touched her hand, let his fingers contract on it. She was not so regal now, for the frightened woman below the crown was showing clearly.

Her plight stabbed into his heart.

There must be something he could do, even now! Bran the Lucky had a reputation to live up to. Always, he had found the one way out of any difficulty. It was a kind of trademark.

His lips curled wryly. There was no escape from this dilemma. The jaws of the trap were sprung too tightly. Somebody had thrown away the key and left them here.

Yet he said softly, to Peganna, "Easy, now! Things are always blackest before the dawn."

The green eyes darted at him as the bloodless lips smiled. "Bran, Bran! As you love me, no false hopes. I–couldn't stand to have them lifted and then broken. As it is, I'm resigned."

The air-car slid on, smoothly, effortlessly.

Taking them to their deaths.

Five hours later, in the white uniform of the Fleet Admiral he had been, Bran Magannon told himself that the Empire did not intend to try a ragged wanderer of the star-ways, at least. They meant him to go out as Admiral Bran Magannon, former High Admiral of Space, with all his campaign ribbons and his many medals splashed across his broad chest. His mirror told him he made a handsome, imposing figure. A hero image.

It was this notion of the hero that Empire wanted to destroy.

The old itch for battle surged into his blood, sending it along his veins in a tidal wave of vitality. Die? The Wanderer? The Lucky One? Ah, no. There was a way out. Somehow, in some manner, there existed the narrow passageway, the legal loophole, through which he and Peganna might slip free. At least, he hoped so.

In his uniform and medals he went to see his counsel.

He found a young man waiting in the hotel suite that was his prison, a pretty girl at his side. The girl was bent over a recording device, a new model with which Bran was unfamiliar, having been so long in the stars. Both the man and the girl rose to their feet when he entered.

Twice the young man cleared his throat. Then he said, "I have been assigned to defend you, Admiral. My name is Randolph Creel. This is Joyle Arrons, my dictographer."

Bran bowed and sat down.

The young man could hold out no hope for acquittal. All he could do was advise Admiral Magannon that he and Queen Peganna must throw themselves on the leniency of the Tribunal. Plead guilty, and make a plea for mercy.

"What mercy?" wondered Bran, and the young lawyer flushed. A moment Bran sat, studying him. "Counselor, many years ago I learned that while the truth may not necessarily be a defense at law, it is better than any lie, no matter how well concocted. We will tell the truth."

"I was afraid you would say that, sir. It's what the queen said, too, when we visited her. I am to defend you both."

"The truth may not be enough," Bran admitted. "It depends on whether we are believed, and even if we are believed, whether it will make any difference in the long run. Now as my lawyer, and as lawyer for the queen, this is what you must do . . ."

Two hours later, a little stiff, the young man rose from his chair. The girl nodded at him, folding up her portable recorder. He would do as the Admiral asked, sending men to Miranor and to Kuleen and to Yvriss, to make depositions and subpoena witnesses.

"Am I to be kept from the queen while we wait trial?" Bran wondered when his visitors were in the corridor doorway.

"Oh, no," the girl said in a rush of words. "Your suite connects with hers through a door at the far side of the fireplace."

"We are not barbarians, Admiral," Creel said with a smile.

The door closed behind them.

The door near the fireplace opened. Peganna came into the room, in a black mist gown set with little seed pearls, her silver hair coiffed on top of her head and framed by a low golden coronal. She was so lovely Bran could only stand and stare at her.

They shall never kill you, Peganna of the Silver Hair! This I vow! As

151

I have saved you on Makkador and on Miranor, so I shall do on Earth!

She gave a little cry and ran into his arms.

When she could speak, she whispered, "They'll have a space-beam hookup by laser to the solar worlds and by hyper-spatial rays to the star colonies. Ten billion people will see and hear us condemned to death."

"Good," said Bran.

"Good?" she wondered, staring up at him.

"Safety lies in numbers, acushla. The more who hear our story, the more there are who may believe it. Public opinion is a mighty force."

Instinctively, Peganna knew public opinion was against them.

One month they waited while Empire gathered its witnesses.

They were treated like royalty, wined and dined in their suite with the richest liqueurs and finest foods the Empire could afford. A variation on the theme of the condemned man eating his hearty last meal, Bran knew, but he drank and ate what they sent him with honest enjoyment. Even Peganna ate when he cajoled her.

From time to time, Randolph Creel would visit them, advising them of his success or the lack of it in securing the witnesses they would need for their defense. It became clear to them, as the month hastened toward its close, that whatever defense he intended to make would not be adequate.

"Empire is very determined to see justice done," he said.

"Justice?" asked Peganna.

"Let me say that Empire is determined to secure a judgment of guilty,

152

then. On all counts, with a mandatory death penalty. They have a battery of counselors, the finest in the whole solar system, working on the case."

"While you work alone," Bran noted.

Creel nodded, looking injured.

I expected no less," Bran said thoughtfully. Then, "Tell me, how is Commander Drexel doing these days?"

The lawyer grinned. "Up and about, with his nose jammed far over to one side of his face. He'll go to plastic surgery, of course–but not until after the trial. I think there's a bit of the vulture in Commander Drexel."

"It could be he's merely worried," Bran remarked. "He thinks I'm something of a wizard, capable of pulling live rabbits out of a wolf's lair."

Peganna leaned forward, torture in her eyes. "The vault of the blue egg? Has Empire taken all the objects inside it?"

Creel drew a deep breath. "For ten years men will work on the vault. It's been sealed off and is guarded now by a complete squadron of the Fleet. They're building a town around it, calling it Treasure City."

"Yes, they would. It will advance their technology a million years. It's the greatest discovery ever made, in the memory of man or Lyanirn."

"Your discovery, your highness," Creel exclaimed eagerly. "I intend to point out to the Tribunal that fact, and suggest that in recompense for the vault, you and Admiral Magannon be allowed your freedom."

Bran shook his head. "It will never work, Empire has the vault. And gratitude is a chancy thing after the gift is made."

Peganna looked at him with death in her face.

The month was at an end.

In an air-car on which was focused the space-vision lenses of ten thousand planets, Peganna of the Lyanir and Admiral Bran Magannon were flown to the Hall of the Star Worlds, to face trial by a jury of their peers, in front of the High Tribunal of the Empire.

They walked through the great rotunda, in the curved walls of which was set a titanic astrarama, with the stars as seen from the northern and southern hemispheres of Earth framed behind glass panes. It seemed to the onlooker that he stood on the rim of space when he looked into those transparent plates. An engineering genius had set tiny pinpoints of radiant matter on magnetic beams, arranged in such a way that the universe lay open for viewing.

The thought touched Bran Magannon that with this trial, all those stars and their worlds hung in the balance. Some thing greater than the lives of a man and a woman was at stake, perhaps even the lives of ten billion billion people.

A fey concept, he told himself, but he was troubled.

They came out of the rotunda into the High Court itself, the seats of which were packed with the rich and famous, here to see judgment done on the man and woman who had threatened their security. One could almost feel the antagonism as their eyes studied the defendants when they came side by side down the aisle and to the raised seats behind the counsel table.

Ten judges in white robes, with the gold star cluster on their fronts, filed in and took their places behind the mahogany bench, on a curved dais.

The Chief Justice signaled for the trial to begin.

ELEVEN

TO BRAN MAGANNON, the trial was an eternity of sound. The voices of the witnesses droned on and on, punctuated by the staccato objections of his trial counsel making points of law. There was the whirr of the recorder that showed the battle with the Lyanir and the great victory which Bran Magannon had won for Empire, followed by the tapes of the appearances he had made before this same High Tribunal, pleading the cause of the Lyanir.

Already, contended the Empire, the seeds of treachery were spouting in the heart and mind of its great High Admiral. To reward him for his past record, they had offered him a professorship, with honors. He had spurned this to go out into the stars, perhaps even then hunting a means to strike back at Empire for refusing to admit the Lyanir into its family of planets.

For ten years, Bran Magannon had wandered.

Then he had met Peganna of the Silver Hair, on Makkador. By some trick of the devil, he had escaped the Empire search for him. He had gone out to the unknown worlds of the people who called themselves Crenn Lir and from the mists of time had wrenched the secrets of their war arsenals.

Not for the benefit of the Empire. Oh, no! To place those weapons into the hands of its deadly enemy. His was the hand that would have given the Lyanir the power to destroy the Empire, to smash its worlds, to annihilate its people, unless they bowed to the yoke of a conqueror.

It was a deadly case the prosecution built.

Even sitting here and knowing the truth, Bran Magannon was impressed by the apparent treachery of his actions. He could understand how they might be misinterpreted by Empire and its people. The marvel of it was that they did not hate him; he realized that their hate was reserved for the woman he loved, for Peganna.

155

Peganna understood it, too. She drooped more and more as the trial went into its second week of testimony. She looked hopeful when Empire admitted that Bran Magannon himself had not sent the 'gram which told Peganna to take the Lyanir off Kuleen to Yvriss, but it was only a momentary thing. In her own mind, she stood convicted.

Randolph Creel did not want to put Bran Magannon on the stand. It was only at his own insistence, when Creel had all but finished for the defense, that he was sworn in.

"Will you tell the Tribunal why you came to Earth to plead for the Lyanir when Queen Peganna held them on Kuleen?" asked his attorney.

"I sought living room for her people, no more."

"You did not send the 'gram that told her to move off-planet?"

"I did not."

"Will you tell the Tribunal about your wanderings?"

"I was heart-sick. I wanted only to be alone with my misery, like a wild animal when it's wounded. I love Peganna of the Silver Hair. I say it now before the billions of people who are watching and listening to this trial on the ten thousand star worlds. What I did, I did for her—and for the good of the Empire.

"She and I found the vault. Not to use it to destroy Empire but intending to offer it with its incredible artifacts in exchange for planets where her people might live in peace with and as allies to my own. Unfortunately, Commander Drexel attacked—invading the sovereignty of an alien world—before we could make our offer."

The court room buzzed with talk. A gavel rose and fell four times, and the commotion stilled.

Bran went on: "The race called the Crenn Lir are our ancestors, those of men and of Lyanir. In a sense, then, the Lyanir are our lost brethren.

Not aliens. Not enemies. Brothers and sisters of the stars.

"We fight now over their heritage. It should be shared alike by all. It is not the property of the Lyanir alone, nor that of Empire. It belongs to both. The Lyanir are in the position of the prodigal son returned home, displaced and dispossessed, instead of having squandered an inheritance. The inheritance is in the vault."

Bran drew a deep breath. "Condemn us, if you will–but grant the people of the Lyanir a place to live, where they will not have to take pills to stay alive! Do this and the queen and I will consider our sacrifice worthwhile."

He talked on, and Peganna wept.

When he was done and he looked into the faces of the ten jurists, he knew his plea had failed. He had offered no new evidence. All he had done was make an explanation, an explanation which in their minds had no weight.

There was no cross-examination.

"The witness will step down," murmured a judge.

The High Tribunal did not leave the bench. There was no need to do so. The judges had reached their verdict before the trial began. They saw no reason to change it now.

"The defendants will please stand," said the Court clerk.

The Chief Justice said softly, "We find the defendants guilty on all counts, on that of treachery in the case of Bran Magannon, on that of conspiracy to attack the Empire in that of Queen Peganna."

There was silence in the courtroom.

Peganna sat like a stone statue for a moment, then she drooped as if the silver hair on her head were an intolerable weight. Bran reached out to put his hand on her arm and when she lifted her face there was misery in its every feature.

Peganna, my heart! As accursed as was Deirdre of the Sorrows!

Bran sat frozen, aware only of his thudding heart and the wildfire in his brain. Fool that he was, not to have seen! Fool! Fool!

A court clerk was calling his name.

"Bran Magannon, have you anything to say to the High Tribunal before judgment is pronounced upon you?"

Bran came easily to his feet. He was a handsome man, still in his white Fleet uniform with all its medals and its ribbons. He squared his shoulders and held his chin high.

"I have! It comes to my mind now that no judgment shall ever be pronounced upon me or upon the queen of the Lyanir."

Peganna gasped and stiffened, staring up at him. The jurists on the high bench stared back at him and somewhere in the courtroom–Bran was certain the voice was that of Commander Alvar Drexel–a man cried out harshly, with disbelief in his throat.

A judge smiled wanly, "Only a miracle can do that."

"Then I bring you a miracle, gentlemen of the Tribunal. Yes, and all you men and women in the star worlds and on Earth itself, and your children and their children after them. I offer you–immortality!"

It was odd in a way, that no one laughed.

His ringing tones went out over the heads of the onlookers and across the vast gulfs of space to the Empire planets, and nowhere did a man hoot, so filled with sudden inspiration was the tongue of Bran Magannon.

"Immortality! For–

"I have found death out there in the stars. A machine on a dead planet that is killing us all–you and me, our sons and our daughters–and I know how to go back to that machine and do what is needed to destroy it."

Utter silence lay like a pall on his shoulders.

Bran said again, "For a long time I didn't know what the machine was. Now I realize it was the weapon of the Yann, put there to kill the Crenn Lir race and you, their descendants. But you need not die. Only give freedom to Peganna of the Silver Hair and set me free as well, and I shall take your war fleet to the planet I named Deirdre and–kill death itself!"

The courtroom was a bedlam. Excited voices rose from every corner. No one heard the Chief Justice with his gavel. Even the men at the space-vision cameras were babbling. Peganna was shaking Bran by the hand, then rising to stand beside him. A light glowed in her green eyes and there was a laugh on her mouth.

"Bran, Bran–is it true? Can you?"

"I can, mavourneen–if the High Tribunal wills it."

Only when the Tribunal threatened to clear the courtroom was there any quiet. Bran could imagine, as he stood with his arm about the waist of Peganna of the Silver Hair, that voices were raised in this same incredible excitement all over the star worlds, in living rooms and salons, in space divers and posh drinking resorts, everywhere that men and women watched the trial.

The Tribunal judges leaned forward as a man.

"Is this possible, Bran Magannon?" one of them asked.

"It is an absolute certainty. To every one looking at me or hearing my voice–everywhere in space–I shall add a thousand years to your lives?"

"Impossible!" a woman screamed. "But–ohh, God! If it were true!"

"Test me," Bran said softly. "Test me for the truth and then decide what you will do. By serum or truth ray–if you care for life and what the future may hold–test whether I speak the truth."

The courtroom sensed that truth in his voice and attitude. It erupted with shouts, with excited voices. This time the High Tribunal could not quiet them, so the Chief Justice made a sign to the clerk, to bring Bran Magannon and the queen of the Lyanir into chambers.

Dusk lay like a purple haze across the Earth as the Solar President rose to his feet when his two visitors came into the Chamber of the Empire. He lifted out of the high-backed chair that was like a throne and moved between the dignitaries of a hundred worlds, reaching out his hands to clasp those of Bran Magannon and Peganna of the Silver Hair.

"The result of the truth tests was flashed to me less than an hour ago," he told them. "I have signed the pardons, giving you both liberty. With it I have incorporated the treaty between Empire and the Lyanir, in which your people, Queen Peganna, and my own, will be allies and as equals. Even now ships are taking off for Miranor to bring your people to the planets we have given them."

Peganna swayed and gasped her thanks.

The Solar President turned his magnetic eyes on Bran Magannon, saying, "With your pardon, I have added clauses restoring to you your rank of High Admiral of Space for Life–no matter how long that life may be."

Bran bowed his head. He walked with Peganna and the President to the three chairs and seated himself.

Then he began to speak of the Crenn Lir.

"They lived a thousand years, each and every one of them, before they were attacked by the Yann. The Yann destroyed all life on their farthermost planet, that I call Deirdre and which they named Ufinisthan and on that planet they put a machine which would have obliterated the Crenn Lir in time, for it shortened their life span to less than a tenth of what it should be. From a thousand years they lived less than half a century because of the rays from that machine that attacks the cellular structure of human bodies.

"When we found traces of dead bodies around the vault on Miranor, they were all of old men because the Yann machine hastened the aging process in the human cells, perhaps by some as yet unknown form of electromagnetic ray. Being close to the machine, the Crenn Lir aged swiftly. Earth and Lyanol are far from those worlds, yet even so the radiation touches us all.

"That radiation may affect the deoxyribonucleic acids in our bodies–the DNA molecules which is the stuff of life itself–destroying it or altering its effectiveness so that the body which depends on it for life is robbed of its inherent properties. I'm not sure of this. It's only my guess. Earth and Lyanirn scientists can study the ray later on and find out what makes it so potent. My only concern is to destroy it. Utterly.

"I don't believe that the Crenn Lir understood just what it was the Yann had done or they would have destroyed the machine themselves. Instead they fled from their worlds in spaceships, seeking to escape the mysterious death that was overcoming them. One or more of those ships reached Lyanol. One or more landed on Earth. Yet even across the vast gulfs of space, the Yann weapons found them. Its rays went everywhere and did their deadly work.

"As a million years passed, the rays weakened. As you know, the human life span has been increasing over the years. Our life expectancy now is a hundred years. In the Twentieth Century, it was only in the sixties.

"Destroy the Yann machine and it will be a thousand, perhaps more. I'll take a fleet out to Deirdre. I'll aim the weapon that will destroy the machine that has taken from us our birthright, with my own hands."

Bran smiled and looked about him. The delegates from the solar and the star planets were quivering with delight. The laser communicators between the Empire planets had been filled to overload with the voices of their people speaking out their minds in 'grams.

Free Bran Magannon! Free Peganna!

In exchange for their freedom, accept their gift!

Bran said, "There are in the holy books, records of men living for long lifetimes. Methuselah, for instance. This may be a recollection of the Crenn Lir days when man did live a thousand years. No one will ever know for sure.

"But I know that man can and will live that long, once Deirdre is rid of the blight that has been bringing us death for a million long years."

The room erupted with applause.

The ambassadors and diplomats of a hundred star world colonies filed forward then, to be introduced to the living legend who was Bran the Lucky, the Wanderer, who was once again High Admiral of the Empire feet. Men grasped his hand and women curtsied, as they bowed and curtsied before Queen Peganna.

There was dancing, with the President claiming Peganna as his First Partner, Bran claiming his wife. Applause blanketed the room as they swung in the stately rhythms of the Star Waltz. Then there were toasts to be drunk, and more speeches listened to, and still more dances.

During the playing of a popular melody, Peganna pressed against Bran, whispering, "Darling, I'm exhausted. Try and get away as soon as possible." Her breath tickled his neck as she added, with a faint smile, "I want to talk over our wedding plans."

"We'll be married when the machine on Deirdre is destroyed, acushla. The President had told me it'll be a state affair, a symbolic joining of our two people. An omen of the peace that has come to both of them."

She pinched his arm. "Before, darling. My heart is set on it"

"After, my heart. Remember, you're a queen."

She was silent, but she had not given in so easily. All the way back to their hotel she argued, and even when they were alone in the suite of rooms assigned them. She pointed out that as rayanal of the Lyanir– which he would be when he married her–he would be serving both the Empire and her people.

Bran said, "I owe it to Empire to perform the act in my official capacity. It's why we were set free. It's why I was given back my command."

Peganna pouted, but Bran was firm.

Finally the queen said, "All right, Bran–we'll throw for it. Your dice, the dice of Nagalang. We'll use those."

Bran grinned and lifted the dice from the pocket of his uniform. "You're making a mistake, Peganna darling. No man can beat me with these things, nor even a woman."

Her chin lifted. "I beat you once in that tavern on Makkador when I wagered the three fame pearls against you."

"Only because I let you, mavourneen. Watch now."

He let the cubes roll about in his palm, making tiny sounds. Peganna caught flashing glimpses of the dragon crests of Tarrn and the cats of Bydd. Then Bran let the dice go across the carpet as he hunkered down.

"I call the cast of a ship of Kriil and a Rim world banner," he said before they stilled their tumbling, and when they were unmoving, a ship and a banner showed. Bran caught the dice in a hand again.

"I'll cast the dragons for you now, my sweet," he laughed.

And he did.

Peganna stared at him. Bran chuckled. "Yes, I lost deliberately to you at the tavern. I've always belonged to you, one way or another, so what was the difference if we made it official?"

He held the dice up so she could see their beauty in the lamplight. "I found them long ago on a star world and I learned after a bit of practice that they responded to my thoughts. There may be a tiny battery of some sort inside each of them that makes them sensitive to brain waves. Or maybe it's the material of the dice themselves."

"Let me roll them," Peganna said thoughtfully.

"I'll make you throw the three stars," he told her as she made her roll.

From the three stars on each die to Bran Magannon, Peganna moved her eyes. For a moment she looked angry, then she laughed.

"As Alvar Drexel said, Bran Magannon always has a way out, that none of us can see." She frowned a moment. "Bran give me the dice as a wedding present. I want to use them when my counselors go against my wishes. I'll give them each a chance to roll against me–and I'll control each roll. By Kronn! I'll be one queen who finds herself obeyed every time."

In the end, it was decided to take one of the weapons of the Crenn Lir out to the planet called Deirdre and with it destroy forever the weapon which had doomed the worlds of their ancestors. It was poetic justice, of a sort.

Admiral Magannon commanded the war-fleet For the first time, Lyanir ships ran nose by nose with the space battle-wagons of the Empire, united under the banners of star cluster and double ax

Peganna of the Silver Hair aimed the weapon, as Bran had taught her to do. She sighted carefully on the glittering metal and touched the protonic transversal. The machine hummed and the Yann weapon was gone.

It no longer existed. It had been hurled instantly into the null universe and since positive matter was diametrically opposed to nullity, it could not exist, as darkness may not exist where there is light.

"It is done," breathed Peganna.

"And the trail is ended, acushla."

Her lips dimpled into a smile as she nestled against him, enjoying his embarrassed stiffness as the officers under his command diplomatically turned away their faces. On board a Fleet warship, even a queen ought to obey the unwritten law, their backs told her as they moved out of the gun port.

Peganna only laughed and hugged him.

"My husband to be," she whispered into his ear, "the future Lord of the Lyanir, its rayanor You're so pompous when you wear that uniform. I liked you better as the Wanderer."

Bran had to smile down at her mischievous face.

"The Wanderer had no dignity to live up to," he told her softly. "He had no home, no wife, no people."

"He will have all of those things now," she murmured.

She opened her arms and Bran stepped into them.

END

Thank you for purchasing Gardner Francis Fox's intergalactic adventure: The Arsenal of Miracles.

Find out more about Mr. Fox by visiting

GARDNERFFOX.com

Printed in Great Britain
by Amazon

15171607R00099